FORGETTING THE BILLIONAIRE

ANNE-MARIE MEYER

❀ Created with Vellum

To my first and only love

CHARLIE

*J*ust Charlie's luck— she was late again. Standing outside the diner, she took a deep breath. Maybe Jorge wouldn't notice this time. Maybe.

If only she hadn't slept in past her alarm. But she had been so tired from the night before. Francis had disappeared again, and Charlie had searched all night, just to find the ninety-five year-old woman hiding in the pantry eating cookies. By the time Charlie had fallen asleep, all she got were three hours of restless slumber. When she finally woke up, she had realized she must have hit the snooze button one too many times, and her shift had already started.

The familiar clang of dishes and silverware greeted her as she pulled open the back door to Jorge's Diner and stepped into the bustling kitchen. The smell of french fries and hamburgers wafted around her.

"Girl, what happened to you?" Priscilla asked as she passed by holding a plate of steaming meat slathered in gravy.

Charlie ran her fingers through her dark brown hair and pulled it up into a bun. Hopefully that helped make her look a bit more presentable. "I was up all night," she said, following after Priscilla who paused at the swinging door.

"Nice," Priscilla said, wiggling her eyebrows.

Charlie rolled her eyes. Leave it to her best friend to turn everything dirty. "It wasn't like that. One of the ladies went missing last night, and I had to search half of Sitka to find her." She leaned against the door frame.

"I told you to sell that place. Why you live with all those old people is beyond me. You're twenty-five. Get a better job." Priscilla sighed as she pushed through the door.

Charlie straightened and opened her mouth to remind Priscilla that she stayed there because it was her grandmother's, and she was fighting to keep it from going under, but Priscilla was already out of earshot. The door swung shut, leaving Charlie alone. It's not like she'd never thought about leaving the place. But every time she did a familiar pain of losing something that was her grandmothers, shot through her chest. No. She couldn't just leave. As crazy as some of the residents were, they needed people in their lives, and she'd be that person.

"You're late," A deep, Spanish accent drawled behind her.

Charlie sucked in her breath and turned.

Jorge stood with his arms crossed in front of his chest, and his forefinger drumming his tanned arm.

"Jorge, I'm so sorry—"

He raised a finger. "Charlie, you promised me three times already that you wouldn't be late anymore." He narrowed his eyes which caused his bushy black eyebrows to squish together. "This is your final warning."

"Yes." She lowered her voice and nodded. There was no way she could afford to lose this job. She was already behind on the mortgage for the retirement home. Not wanting him to change his mind about letting her have another chance, she dashed to the back wall where the rusty lockers were located and pulled out her apron. Tying the strings around her waist, she pushed through the swinging door.

The dining room was in full lunch swing. All the metal tables were filled with locals and fishermen that were in Sitka to take advantage of the King Salmon that filled the waters. Priscilla was chatting with a few of them as Charlie approached her. She giggled and swatted the arm of a beefy fisherman. Charlie rolled her eyes. Always the flirt.

"Which tables haven't you covered?" she asked.

Priscilla waved her hand toward the back wall and continued her obvious flirting.

Charlie followed her gesture. Sitting with his back toward her, was a man in a dark suit with his head down. He stuck out like a sore thumb in this room full of baseball caps and plaid button-ups. She grabbed the pad out of her pocket and walked up, forcing a smile as she approached. "Hi. Welcome to Jorge's Diner. What can I get for you today?"

The man was consumed with his phone. His finger scrolled the screen. He sighed and glanced over at her, and his sky-blue eyes narrowed. "It's about time," he said.

He only looked a few years older than her. His blond hair was tousled, but in an intentional way. His gaze ran over her, instantly making her feel self-conscious. She didn't recognize him which meant this man was a tourist. In and out. That was life on an island.

Taken aback by his coldness, Charlie swallowed. "I'm sorry?"

The man tucked his phone into his suit coat and waved to the table. "I haven't even gotten a menu yet. I'd leave, but this seems to be one of the only places to eat in this forsaken city."

He was rude. She fought the urge to tell him off. Instead, she brushed off his comment with an awkward laugh. Sitka was small, but beautiful. "I'm sorry. I just started my shift. Let me get you a menu." She shoved the pad back into her apron pocket and nodded toward the cash register. She would've told him what she thought, but she was already skating on thin ice with Jorge as it was.

The muscles in the man's jaw flexed as his gaze swept over her. "Thanks."

She hurried over to the counter and grabbed a menu. Silently, she prayed that this one didn't have gravy on it. She gave it a quick once over before handing it to him. He took it between two fingers and opened it up.

Like an idiot, she waited for a thank you, but it never came. She turned to leave, but he raised his hand and brushed her arm. A shiver raced across her skin. Anger and excitement flitted through her stomach. Instantly, she stopped, frustrated with what his touch did to her.

"Miss, I'm ready."

"Charlie," she said. It was an instinct. She hated being called "miss".

"What?"

"The name. It's Charlie." Brushing her apron down, she glanced over to him.

The man widened his eyes as he studied her. "Okay, Charlie. I'll get the burger with fries."

She jotted down his order. "Did you want it slathered?"

His nose crinkled. "Slathered?"

Her cheeks heated. "Means you want it with all the fixings. Lettuce, tomatoes, onions, mayo—"

He nodded his head. "Sure," he said with annoyance in his voice. He raised the menu to her.

"Okay." She pinched her lips to stop herself from saying anything more and took the menu from him. Back in the kitchen, she leaned against the wall as the door swung closed, separating her from the mysterious man. She rested her head back as she took a deep breath.

What was with her today? It seemed everyone was upset with her. She had managed to tick off every guy she had come across.

She could understand Jorge being upset with her, but this customer? What was his problem?

The door swung open nearly hitting her. Priscilla's high-pitched laugh rang in her ears. Heat pricked her neck. She needed to get it together.

"Charlie, what're you doing back there?" Priscilla asked as the door closed.

Charlie took a few deep breaths. She needed to get her emotions under control before she lost it. "Sorry. The guy you saved for me is a real piece of work."

Priscilla handed the order over to Samuel who was camped out at the grill and turned. "I kind of kept the table of hotties for myself. Sorry."

Charlie shrugged. She wasn't even up for small talk, much less flirting right now. "It's okay." She handed her order over to Samuel who grunted and took it.

She followed Priscilla over to the fountain drinks and filled up a glass with ice water for the mysterious and rude man.

"Who is he?" Priscilla asked as she peeked through the circular window on the swinging door.

Charlie shrugged. "Never met him. Tourist most likely."

A wide smile spread across Priscilla's lips. "Ooo, that's the best. No attachments. It's perfect for you. Maybe you can finally forget..." She raised her eyebrows as if that was the new name for Charlie's ex-boyfriend.

Frustrated at the mention of him, Charlie ripped the bottom of the straw wrapper off with a bit more gusto than normal. "Alex. You can say his name. It's Alex."

Priscilla raised her hands. "I wasn't sure. For a while it was synonymous with Voldemort."

"It was a year ago, and I'm over it." Charlie's voice came out higher than intended. She slammed her lips shut. That was not the sound of someone who'd gotten over her three-year relationship.

Priscilla noticed, and sympathy filled her gaze.

"I'm over him." Charlie narrowed her eyes, but Priscilla's expression didn't change. Groaning, she grabbed the water and stomped out of the kitchen.

What did Priscilla know? Charlie left Alex after she caught him making out with another girl. She bit her lower lip. She was better off without him. Right?

"Ahh!" A yell pulled Charlie from her thoughts. The red face of the rude man shot into her line of vision.

"Wha—"

"You dumped that water in my lap," he growled as he swiped at his now soaked pants.

Charlie's face heated as she stared at the large water spot. Somehow she'd managed to miss the table and dumped the entire glass of ice water onto him. Mortified, she grabbed a nearby napkin and leaned in to start dabbing. "I'm so—"

"Excuse me!" He reached down and pulled the napkin from her hand.

Her skin burned as she realized just what part of him she had zoned in on to dab. "Oh, my gosh, I'm so sorry." She avoided his gaze which she was sure was raging by now.

"This suit was from Italy! Do you know how much it cost me?"

His anger rang in her ears as she searched for more napkins. After unrolling a few bundles of silverware, she handed them over. "Really. I'm so sorry." She met his gaze. His blue eyes had turned stony as he took the napkins from her and continued to dab.

"I'm so sorry, sir. What happened?" Jorge asked from behind her.

Charlie's stomach sank. She turned to meet his angry gaze.

"*She* dumped water on my lap," the man said. Charlie could feel him stare at her.

"I apologize. That is not how we do things. Charlie, you are excused from helping this man. Go back to the kitchen."

Tears pricked at her eyes as she nodded. She didn't want to cry in front of this man or Jorge. Why did she even get out of bed? She should have stayed under her covers for the rest of her life. From the look on Jorge's face, he wasn't going to be very forgiving this time. She pushed through the kitchen door and stood in the corner, biting her lip.

A few minutes ticked by, but it felt like an eternity. Finally, the door swung open, and Jorge entered.

"Charlie," he started as he glanced over at her.

"Jorge, I'm so sorry. It was an accident. I promise it will never happen again. Please, you have to believe me," she stammered.

He raised his hand causing Charlie to pinch her lips shut. This was never good.

"I just think you've been extremely distracted lately. It might be time for us to reevaluate your position here. Perhaps, it would be better if you took some time off." Jorge studied her.

With each word, Charlie's stomach sank further and further. The retirement home depended on her income to stay afloat. If she was fired, what would she do? What would the residents do?

"Jorge, I promise that will never happen again." She was desperate. She debated getting on her knees and begging, and she'd do it if she thought it would change his decree.

He shook his head. "I've already made the decision. Your final check will be available in a week." He folded his arms over his chest. His signature *this conversation is done* move.

Anger and frustration boiled up inside of her, but all she could do was nod. Her job here was finished. She handed over her apron, walked over to her locker, and pulled open the door. Grabbing her purse and odds and ends, she slammed the door and turned. The kitchen had been silent for their conversation, but the noise had resumed.

Not wanting to stay in this horrible place any longer, Charlie pushed open the back door and stepped out. It had started drizzling. Yet another gloomy day, and she welcomed the grey sky. Rounding the corner, she slammed right into someone who was tucked under the building's awning. He turned, pulling a phone from his ear.

"Ah, not you," she muttered when she realized it was the rude man from inside. For once, she was thankful that she was drenched in rain. He wouldn't be able to see the tears that threatened to spill from her eyes.

He glanced at her as he reached up and ran his fingers through his damp hair. "That wasn't my intention."

She narrowed her eyes and shook her head. She was too exhausted to try and figure out what he meant. "What?"

He nodded toward the diner. "To get you fired. That wasn't my intention."

Anger boiled up inside. "Well you should have thought about that before you acted like a complete jerk." He was no longer her customer. She didn't have to be nice to him. Two could play at this game. She folded her arms and narrowed her eyes.

He leaned back, almost as if he were surprised she had said that to him. She scoffed. There had to have been other people who talked to him like that. Or maybe she just brought out the loser in every guy she met.

"You could have told him it was an accident. I needed that job. Did you even think of that?" She was on a roll now. Plus, he was silent. She glared at him as she stepped around him. "Next time, act like a human and have some decency. Who raised you?" Too scared to look back, Charlie kept walking. Her final words lingered in the air.

The farther she got away from him, the better she felt. Served him right. After what he did, she was proud of herself for telling him how she felt. She was done getting walked over. As she made her way down the familiar streets, she couldn't help but smile. It felt good to finally say what was on her mind. Even if it was to man she'd never see again, it was a start.

2

MITCHELL

"*A*re you even listening to word I'm saying?"

Mitchell brought the phone back to his ear as he watched Charlie, the intriguing waitress, stomp down the street. A smile twitched on his lips as he noted her confident strut. She seemed very proud of herself for telling him off. Maybe he deserved it.

"What, Victoria?" he asked as he pulled his gaze back to the ground and focused on the woman on the other end.

"I said, are you listening to me?"

"Yes." He lied. Why had she called him? She knew he needed some space right now.

"Really?" she asked.

"Um hum."

"I don't understand why you had to go up there. What's in Alaska anyways?"

Mitchell sighed as he leaned against the diner's brick exterior. They'd already had this conversation. "My grandmother is up here." He accentuated each word. Perhaps he needed to say it slower so it would sink in.

"But I miss you."

He clenched his jaw. So much for being the supportive girl-friend figure. Why did Victoria have to make everything about her? "So, there's no emergency?" He decided to move this conversation forward.

"I'd say missing you was an emergency."

"Vic, listen, I'm here to visit my grandma. I'll see you when I get back." He hit the end call button, but not before he heard her whimpering on the other end. Maybe he needed to reevaluate his choice in women.

He shoved his phone into his coat pocket and made his way back into the restaurant. His burger and fries were cold. He considered complaining, but let it go. He'd already gotten one person fired today. No need to do it again.

"Do you need anything else?" The cold voice of the other waitress broke his thoughts.

"I'm okay." He couldn't help but notice that she was glaring at him. "You okay?"

She ripped a piece of paper from her pad and let it fall to the table. "You got my best friend fired. You tell me."

He felt bad. It really hadn't been his intention. It was this trip. It'd turned him into a monster. After he received the call that his grandma had only weeks to live, he got on his plane and flew straight here. Now, he was trying to bring himself to go see her, but he was struggling more than he'd thought. He even instructed his pilot, Pedro, to hang out at the airport just in case he needed a quick getaway.

"Really. I am sorry. Could you let her know if you see her?"

The waitress narrowed her eyes as she grabbed the twenty he'd laid down and nodded. After she stalked off, he stood and walked over to the door. Thankfully, his pants had dried somewhat. It no longer looked as if he'd peed himself. Stepping outside, he made his way to his rental car.

It was a VW bug— the only car they had left at the rental place. The worst part was that it was pink. He felt ridiculous driving around in it. But buying a brand-new car just to be here for a few days seemed a bit ridiculous, so he gritted his teeth and took it.

He slipped inside and started the engine. And sat there with his hands gripping the steering wheel. He watched as the rain hit the windshield and rolled down. It had been less than twenty-four hours since he got the call that brought him here.

Why his grandma had insisted on retiring on this tiny island was beyond him. What was so great about Sitka? His gaze pushed past the rain and up to the trees that reached toward the sky. She'd lived the rest of her life so far away from family— far away from him. And now? He didn't want to even think the words, but they pounded in his skull anyways. *She was going to die here.*

His stomach twisted.

A piercing sound filled the air. He jumped and glanced around. Vibration rattled his chest. He patted his pocket. It was his phone. Reaching inside his suit coat, he hit the talk button and brought it to his ear. Probably Victoria calling again.

"Hello?"

"Mitchell?" The familiar uptight voice caused him to grit his teeth.

"Mother?"

"Thank goodness I caught you. I've been trying to call you all day. I'm downstairs and coming up."

He twisted the grasp he had on the steering wheel. "I'm not home right now."

"What?" she scoffed. "That's ridiculous. Where else would you be?"

Mitchell swallowed and braced himself. She was not going to like what he was about to tell her. "I'm in Sitka."

Silence.

"Alaska," he continued.

"I know where Sitka is. Why are you there?"

"Don't you mean, why am I seeing her?"

She cleared her throat. "This family's relationship with her was over a long time ago, Mitchell Kingsley. Why have you gone against my wishes?"

"Mother, I'm not part of this feud. My relationship isn't over. The fact that you kept her location a secret from me all this time is horrible."

More silence.

"She's dying, Mom." A lump formed in his throat. Since he was a baby, his grandma Rose had raised him. While his parents were off growing their business, she was the one who taught him to tie his shoes and play baseball. She always insisted on raising him humble despite his family's wealth. But after the incident, his parents severed all ties.

"I know." His mom's voice had turned to ice.

He stared at the drizzling rain. Rage filled his chest. His mother knew Rose was sick and she wasn't even going to come? Why was he here and still sitting in the parking lot? He threw the car in reverse and pulled onto the road.

"I need to go, Mom." He slammed the end call button and threw his phone onto the passenger seat. After a few left turns, he admitted he was lost, so grabbed his phone and punched in the location of Dottie's Retirement Home.

Ten minutes later he pulled into the back lot of a small red house. It had white painted shutters with window boxes that exploded with flowers. A porch wrapped all the way around with a few rockers scattered throughout.

He took a deep breath and opened the car door. Leaving his luggage in the car, he raced across the gravel and up to the porch steps. A woman with frizzy white hair sat in a chair, staring at him.

"Hello," he said as he nodded to her.

The woman's gaze looked hopeful. "Kenny?"

Mitchell brushed some water droplets off his suit. He was just going to throw it away when he got home. "Sorry, no. I'm Mitchell."

She scrunched her nose. A car drove by, drawing her attention toward the street.

Mitchell felt bad as he made his way to the front of the house. He wished he could talk with her more. She seemed lonely. Maybe later. Right now, he was on a mission.

Opening the front door, he stepped inside. He stood in a small mud room where five cubbies were overflowing with coats and hats. He swiped the rain from his suit one more time, hoping to look presentable. The door swung shut behind him, and its thud caused him to jump. There was no going back now.

Loud salsa music from down the hall drew his attention. He wiped the bottom of his shoes on the front mat and walked toward the closed door. Not sure what to do, he knocked. When no one answered, he knocked again.

"Hello?" he called out.

A laugh broke out from the other side. It was sweet against the spicy music.

Turning the door handle, he pushed. The kitchen was small and painted with bright yellows and oranges. Colorful dishes were displayed against one wall while aged appliances were sandwiched along another. All the furniture had been pushed to the side to allow for more space.

"I knocked, but no one answered," Mitchell said as he stepped further into the room. Suddenly, a woman spun out in front of him. Startled, he reached out and caught her.

Another giggle. "I'm so sorry—"

He glanced down and realized why she'd stop talking.

"Charlie?" he asked, but then instantly felt stupid. Was it still okay if he called her by her first name? He did just get her fired.

"Rude guy?" She pushed off his chest and took a few steps back.

"Mitchell," he corrected.

She brushed down her skirt. She must be nervous. He'd seen her do that at the diner earlier.

"Why are you here?" She narrowed her eyes.

"Why are *you* here?"

Her face reddened. "I work here."

He glanced around. "You work here and the diner?"

"Well, not the diner. Not since you got me fired."

Heat crept up his neck. "Right, about that. I didn't mean—"

"To get me fired. I know. You said that already." She made her way to far corner where an elderly man stood. "Where were we, Floyd? Before we were so rudely interrupted."

She stepped up to him, and they joined hands. His weathered skin wrinkled as he grinned at her.

"M'lady," he said as he reached around and placed his hand on her back.

"Come on," she said, smiling and resting her hand on his shoulder.

Floyd leaned forward, and Charlie moved with him. Soon, they were dancing around the kitchen. Not knowing what to do, Mitchell leaned against the far counter and watched. Charlie's long brown hair had been freed from the confines of the bun she'd had it in earlier, and it swayed with her movements.

Who was this woman? The softness of her curves as she moved across the kitchen caused his heart to pound. He clenched his jaw. He was here to see his grandmother, that was all. He needed to get his head on straight and focus.

The song ended, and Charlie led Floyd over to a nearby chair. Then she walked over to the radio and turned the music down. Feeling unsure of what to say, Mitchell fiddled with his phone. There was something about her that unnerved him, and he wasn't sure why.

"So, what do you want? Trying to get me fired from here as well?" she asked as she glanced over at him.

He cleared his throat and slipped his phone back into his pocket. Why were his palms so sweaty? It must be the humid Alaskan air. "I'm here to see a resident."

She filled a glass with water and took a drink. Her dark brown eyes never left his face. "That's specific," she said when she lowered the glass.

"Rose McDermont?"

Her gaze softened. "Are you a relative?"

He nodded. "I'm her grandson."

Charlie placed the glass on the counter and rested both hands next to it. Her shoulders rose as if she were taking deep breaths.

"Is she...is she okay?" Why was she acting this way? Did she have bad news?

Charlie pushed off the counter and turned. Suddenly, a searing pain shot through his cheek. The impact threw his face to the side. She slapped him! Why did she slap him? He righted himself and glanced over at her. "What the—"

"That's for getting me fired and for not coming to see her sooner. What's with your family? It's like no one cared that she was getting worse." Her hands shook as she grasped the one she had just slapped him with.

He rubbed his cheek as he stared at her. "I didn't know. It wasn't until yesterday that I even found out that she was here, much less sick."

Her angry gaze softened as his words sank in. "Wait. What?"

"You've been calling my mom. They don't talk anymore. That's why no one answered. Believe me, I would've come sooner."

"Oh." Her face reddened as she raced over to the freezer and grabbed a few ice cubes. One fell to the ground as she made her way over to him.

He held out his hand as she dropped them onto his palm. Their coolness shocked his skin.

"I... I didn't know. I'm sorry. My emotions have been everywhere today."

Mitchell just nodded as he brought the cubes to his cheek. "It's okay. I guess I deserved that. I mean, I did get you fired."

"That's true." A smile twitched on her lips.

Her perfectly formed pink lips. He dropped his gaze and focused on the ice on his cheek. He shouldn't be staring at her lips. "Is she okay?" Saying something seemed like a good idea. It'd help get his thoughts off of Charlie's mouth.

The smile disappeared. "Come on," she said and turned toward the door he'd just entered. "I'll be back Floyd," she called over her shoulder.

The man nodded as he turned the page of the newspaper he was reading.

Dread filled Mitchell's chest as he followed her. This couldn't be good. What would Rose say? What would she think? He'd been absent from her life for so long, he had little hope she'd forgiven his family. Words once spoken could never be taken back. It'd take time to restore the relationship that was broken. At this moment, from the look on Charlie's face, he doubted he had that kind of time.

3

CHARLIE

*H*e was here. Walking right behind her. The man that she'd yelled at behind the diner was here. And she'd slapped him. What was the matter with her?

Rose. That's right. That's why her emotions were so raw. Rose was the person who'd taken the place of her grandmother when she'd passed away. The woman who was now slipping from Charlie's grasp. The woman who had wanted nothing more than to be surrounded by her family as her life deteriorated.

Charlie swallowed to still her frustration and led Mitchell up the creaking steps to the second floor. At the top, she took a left. Doors lined either side of the hall. Most residents were mobile enough to move around. They stayed at this home that her grandmother had started to enjoy the retired life.

Only two of them had memory issues— Francis and Rose. They also happened to be the two women Charlie was fighting so hard to keep here. They were her grandmother's best friends and basically aunts to her.

The Alaskan light spilled through the window at the far end of the hall. At the moment, the clouds had parted giving Sitka a few glimpses of sun. She stopped outside Rose's door, and Mitchell stood a foot away. She could feel his presence.

Charlie stilled her nerves. It was hard to walk into Rose's room every day. For some reason, having Mitchell so close to her eased that pain. She tilted her head and glanced over at him. He was staring at the door with a mixture of hurt and frustration across his face.

He seemed as broken as she felt. And she'd smacked him. Gah. She could be such an idiot sometimes. A hot-headed girl, that's what her grandmother had always called her.

"She's in here," Charlie said as she reached out and turned the handle.

Warmth engulfed her fingers. Mitchell had reached out, stilling her hand. Startled, she glanced over at him. His blue eyes were stormy and sad. As her gaze ran down his face, she felt her breath catch in her throat. He was hands down one of the most handsome men she'd ever seen.

"Wait," he finally spoke with painful emotion filling his voice.

She watched as his gaze slipped to their grasped hands then up to her. He released her hand as if he had suddenly realized they were touching.

"Could you... could you go in there and let her know I'm here?" His voice dropped with each word. "See if she wants to see me?"

Her hand felt cold from the absence of his. "She's not very lucid anymore." A sharpness stabbed her heart as she spoke the words.

Mitchell pressed his lips together and nodded. From the look in his eyes, he was unable to form any words to speak.

Twisting the handle, Charlie opened the door and walked inside. The far curtains had been opened, and she let out a sigh. That was a positive sign. It meant today was a good day.

"Hello," a honey sweet voice greeted her.

Charlie made her way farther into the room to see Rose sitting on her bed. She had her hair out of curlers, and her grey hair framed her face. Her makeup was on, and she was dressed. It even looked as if some of the clothes that were normally strewn around the room had been picked up.

"How are you this afternoon?" Charlie asked, giving her the biggest smile she could muster.

"Well, I'm fine. Thanks for asking." Rose placed the book that was in her hands down onto her lap.

"You're up." Charlie nodded toward her.

Rose removed the reading glasses that were perched on her nose. "Well, yes. A respectable person does not spend the whole day in her pajamas."

Charlie studied her. Was it Rose? Had she come back?

"Who are you, my dear?" Rose looked confused. There was no recognition there.

Charlie's heart sank at those five words. The worst sentence anyone had ever spoken to her. It meant Rose wasn't here.

"It's Charlie. You know, Charlie?" Even after all this time, she hoped that just reminding Rose would jog her memory.

Rose shook her head. "I'm sorry. I don't know you. Are you Tyler's girl?" A hopeful look flitted across her face.

Charlie fought the tears that formed on the edge of her eyelids. "No. I'm Dottie's granddaughter."

"Who's Dottie?"

Charlie wanted to scream that Dottie was Rose's best friend. That they'd been inseparable for years. Charlie wanted to force out this horrible disease and bring back the woman who was her only link to her grandmother. But none of that anger did any good. It didn't change the illness.

"There's someone here to see you." Charlie forced a smile again. Maybe Mitchell could bring her back.

"Oh? Is it Tyler?" Rose looked hopefully toward the door.

"No, it's your grandson."

"Grandson? Honey, do I look old enough to be a grandmother?" She smiled as if that thought was completely insane. Then, her face grew serious as her gaze slipped to the door. Charlie turned to see what she was looking at.

Mitchell had crept into the room and was staring at Rose.

"Tyler," Rose breathed as she reached out her hand. "You came." She choked as a tear ran down her cheek.

Mitchell turned to Charlie with worry written all over his face. Charlie could only shrug. There was nothing she could do.

"Well, come here and give your mother a hug. You're not too old to do that." Rose opened her arms and waved him over.

He hesitated but complied.

Their embrace made Charlie feel as if she were intruding in on their moment. She turned, but not before she saw Mitchell step back and Rose cradle his cheek with her hand.

"I've missed you," she whispered.

"Grandma, I'm not Tyler. I'm Mitchell," he said, his voice gruff with emotion.

Charlie couldn't go through this again. She backed out towards the door. A loud thunk sounded behind her. Her face reddened as she whipped around to find that she'd knocked a large decorative vase over. Feeling sheepish, she turned back around to see Rose and Mitchell staring at her.

"Who'd you bring to see me, Tyler?" Rose turned back to Mitchell and gave him a huge smile. "Is this the girl?"

"Girl? Tyler? Grandma, you know I'm your grandson," he said.

Rose waved her hand in his direction obviously ignoring him. "There's no need to be embarrassed. Come here, sweetheart. Tyler's always been shy." She reached out her hand for Charlie to take.

Mitchell's eyes widened as he pleaded with her to do something.

Rose smiled at Charlie. "Tyler's told me so much about you," she said.

This was the first time in a long time that Rose was actually looking at her as if she knew exactly who Charlie was, and Charlie had forgotten what that felt like.

Not knowing what else to do, she approached the bed and embraced her. The familiar smell of Rose's perfume filled her nose. When she pulled away, Rose grasped her hand.

"It's so nice to finally meet you." Rose smiled at Mitchell. "You never told me she was so beautiful."

It was subtle, but it looked as if Mitchell blushed as he glanced over at Charlie. But that only lasted until he turned his attention back to Rose.

"Grandma, I already—"

"I am not your grandmother! Do I look old enough to be a grandma?" Rose's voice sharpened as she stared at him.

Mitchell glanced over at Charlie and the pleading returned.

There was only one option that Charlie saw.

"Men." She rolled her eyes and smiled over at Rose. "It's so nice to finally meet you as well. Tyler's told me so much about you, too." She made her way over to Mitchell whose jaw flexed as he stared at her.

Rose giggled. "Men never get a woman's age right." Her admiring gaze had returned. "Grandmother. That's the worst one yet."

Charlie stood next to Mitchell and bit her cheek. How would he react to what she was about to do? Before she lost her nerve, she reached down and grasped his hand. He stiffened next to her.

Rose beamed. "Look at the two of you. Don't you make a beautiful couple?"

"What are you doing?" Mitchell whispered.

Charlie forced a smile and leaned over. "It's what she needs. Go with me on this."

She could feel his stare on her, but she just turned her attention back to Rose.

"Fine," he whispered, but his stance never softened.

"How long are you visiting for?" Rose asked.

Charlie glanced over at Mitchell who looked as if he had eaten something sour.

"Please say a while," Rose pleaded.

When it seemed that Mitchell wasn't going to respond, Charlie squeezed his fingers to nudge him. His gaze returned to her.

"Sweetheart, how long are we going to be here?" Charlie asked, glancing over at him.

His shoulders slumped. "I wasn't— oh, a week," he said as Charlie tightened her grasp.

Rose looked elated. "That's wonderful. Please join me for dinner tonight?"

"Wha—"

"We'd love to." Charlie interrupted as her heart sang. It'd been such a long time since Rose had wanted to leave her room. There was no way Charlie was going to let him mess things up.

"We'd what?" Mitchell asked.

"See you at seven?" Charlie ignored him. She didn't want Rose to change her mind.

Rose smiled. "Brilliant."

Charlie leaned in. "It was nice to meet you, Rose."

Rose nodded and picked up her book and glasses. She looked tired so Charlie decided not to push her further.

"Come on," she said to Mitchell and pulled him from the room.

Once the door was shut, Mitchell turned to her. "What was that?" he said, waving his hand toward the closed door.

She shrugged. "It's what Rose wanted."

He scrubbed his face. "But it's a lie. All of it. I'm not Tyler, and you're not my girlfriend."

Charlie chewed her bottom lip. "I know that. Who's Tyler anyways?"

Suddenly, the red carpet that ran the length of the hall seemed very interesting to him. He brushed it with the toe of his shoe. "My dad," he whispered.

There was something in his countenance that told Charlie not to push the topic. It must have to do with the history that had torn the family apart. Rose never spoke of it either.

As Charlie took in his pain, it fanned her desire to comfort him. She shook her head. That might get a bit awkward. She folded her arms so she didn't reach out.

"Listen, I know this is hard for you. I don't know the history, but I do know that this means a lot to Rose. Can you do this? Please?" How hard was it for him to pretend to be her boyfriend for one dinner? "I mean, unless you have a hot girlfriend back home."

His gaze flew to her face.

Oh. Well that answered that question. "Well, I'm sure she won't mind you doing this to help your grandmother feel better."

He raised his eyebrow.

Charlie paused. "Okay, maybe she will. But it's not like it's real." She grew serious. "I've known your grandmother for a long time. It's been months since I've seen her so interested in something. Please, do this for her. She doesn't have that…" She couldn't bring herself to finish those last few words.

"A dinner?" He turned his gaze to her.

"Yes."

He took in a deep breath. "I can do dinner."

Mitchell stuck around for a few minutes longer, but then left stating he might as well stay the night so needed to secure a hotel room. Now alone, Charlie sat at the kitchen table staring at the dark wood top. She chewed her bottom lip and allowed her gaze to fall to her left. The mound of unopened envelopes that she had dumped onto the table moments ago taunted her.

Sighing, she pulled her hair back up into a bun and slid the bills over until they were right in front of her.

Just like a bandage— rip it off, she chanted in her head.

The back door slammed shut, causing her to jump.

Penny walked in, shaking off her umbrella. "Hey, honey," she exclaimed, hanging her jacket on a hook and stepping into the kitchen. She patted her pure white hair, adjusting the places that the wind had touched.

Penny had worked at the house for as long as Charlie could remember. Her grandmother had given her room and board in exchange for help with the residents. After she passed away, Charlie was more than happy to have Penny stay on.

"How was the beauty shop?" Charlie asked. She leaned against her chair, grateful for the distraction. Anything to provide distance between herself and the responsibility that loomed over her.

Penny made her way over to the cupboard and pulled out the kettle and tea bags. "Tea?" she asked as she turned on the water.

Charlie nodded. "Sure."

Once the kettle was on the stove, Penny took the seat next to her.

"That's quite the pile of mail," she said, eyeing the bills.

Heat crept up Charlie's cheeks. "Yeah."

"Want some help?"

Charlie shook her head. She didn't want the residents to know just how bad things were. She was going to fix this. There had to be a way. "Naw. It's pretty boring."

Penny raised her eyebrows. She had a look that said she didn't believe her.

The whistle of the kettle rang in the air, and Charlie leapt from the table. "I'll get it."

"Charlie," Penny said in a voice that meant she knew Charlie was leaving out details. Charlie's grandma had used the same tone.

Smacking a tea packet against her palm, Charlie refused to turn around. "Really, Penny, it's nothing." After ripping open the packaging, she filled two mugs and dipped the bags into the water.

When she turned, she caught Penny staring at her. She could

feel her suspicion through her gaze. Brushing it off, Charlie set a mug down in front of Penny and returned to her seat.

They each blew on the steam that rose from the water.

Penny set her mug down and turned. "You know, your granny never intended this place to be a burden for you. She knew it had been your home since you were a child and lord knows, she loved the residents here, but she always wanted to see you go and make something of yourself."

Tears brimmed the edge of Charlie's lids. "But, Penny..."

Her weathered hand reached across the table and enveloped Charlie's. "I know you're as stubborn as your granny and you'll do what you want. I'm just telling you, it's okay to let some things go."

Charlie's heart twisted at the words. How could she let go? This was the place her grandmother had built. She'd only been gone less than a year and already Charlie had run it into the ground. What did that say about her?

Taking a sip of the steaming tea, the heat pierced Charlie's throat. She could never leave this place. She'd stay until it was saved.

4

MITCHELL

"*I*'m sorry. Could you repeat that?" Mitchell asked as he stood at the front desk of the Black Bear Motel, staring at a man with thick rimmed glass. He was trying to process what the man had just said.

"I already told you. We don't have any rooms available."

"Why? Who'd come here? Full?" His emotions were still raw from seeing Rose, and he wasn't in the mood for this. He needed a shower and to relax before his dinner appointment.

The man raised his eyebrows as he stared at Mitchell. "Plenty of people. Evidence—we're full."

"Listen, I'll pay anything. Just get me a room."

Apparently, that was the wrong thing to say. The clerk leaned forward as he jutted out his finger. "Sir, I'm sure things are done differently in the lower forty-eight but here, we honor our reservations. It's how we keep repeat customers."

"But—"

"Sir, I'm gonna have to ask you to leave." The man waved his hand toward the door.

Mitchell glanced outside and ran his hands through his hair as his frustration boiled over. He was about to offer the man three times the cost of a room, but when he turned around, the man was gone.

Grabbing the handle of his suitcase, Mitchell dragged it out to the drizzling rain. He picked it up and raced over to his rental. Once inside, he brushed the droplets off his clothes and turned his attention outside. What was he going to do now?

The Black Bear Motel had been the last place to check. Every other motel was booked as well. Apparently, there was a big music festival happening this weekend and all the rooms had been reserved for months. Every clerk had turned him away. Even when he offered them a substantial amount of money. This community was too small. It was strange when honor trumped cash.

Gripping the steering wheel, Mitchell turned the key and the car started up.

"Dottie's Retirement Home," he said to his phone. He had no choice. There was no other place for him to go.

The phone responded and in ten minutes, he was parked behind the red house as he'd done before. He shut off the car and grabbed his luggage. He'd hoped Charlie would be hospitable. As he raced up the back steps his heart quickened. There had been something there when she had grabbed his hand. A feeling he couldn't describe.

Mitchell shook his head. What was he? Fifteen? He didn't get crushes. Besides, he had Victoria. She had all but scheduled the wedding date.

When he got to the front door, he pulled it open and entered. The house was quiet. A dim light cast shadows across the floor of the study on the left. Bookshelves lined the far wall. Three worn arm chairs sat in a circle in the middle of the room. The decorations were dated. This didn't seem like a home of someone in their twenties.

Two voices carried out from the kitchen. The door was open so Mitchell made his way toward it.

He picked out Charlie's instantly. It was young and sweet. The second voice was older. Standing in the door frame, Mitchell glanced around.

Charlie was sitting at the table that had been dragged back to the center of the kitchen. She had her legs pulled up with a mug balanced on one knee. Her hair was back up in a bun. The woman next to her was older. She had white hair and was laughing.

"Hi again," Mitchell said, stepping into the room.

Charlie jumped slightly as she turned to face him. Her eyes widened as her gaze whipped to the clock. "I thought we had agreed on later," she said, setting the mug down and standing. "I haven't even started dinner yet."

Mitchell raised his hand. "No. You said seven. It's just that, well, I've been to every motel in Sitka, and they're all booked. Something about a festival this weekend."

"Oh," Charlie said, glancing over to the other woman.

The older woman nodded and smiled. "That sounds about right. And you are?"

"Penny, I'm sorry, this is Mitchell. Rose's grandson," Charlie said as she brought her mug over to the sink.

Penny's eyebrow furrowed as she ran her gaze over him. "About time, huh?"

Mitchell opened his mouth to reply, but Charlie beat him to it.

"No, it's not like that. Apparently, he just found out that Rose was even here. He came right away."

Penny glanced at Charlie then back to him. "Well, it's nice to meet you then."

"Penny's been helping out around here since I can remember," Charlie said as she leaned against a nearby counter and folded her arms.

"Nice to meet you." Mitchell nodded, and Penny returned it with a smile.

"So, what are you going to do?" Charlie motioned toward his suitcase.

He cleared his throat. "I was hoping I could get a room here. If you don't mind."

Charlie's face flushed as she narrowed her eyes. Mitchell studied her. What did that mean?

"I'm… well…" she turned her gaze over to Penny.

"How long do you need a place?" Penny asked.

"I'm kind of taking it day by day." Mitchell glanced over at Charlie who had her lips pinched together.

"I don't think that should be a problem. Do you, Charlie?" Penny asked, glancing over at her.

Charlie shook her head then paused. Then she started to nod. "I just don't think that this is such a good idea. Booked? All of them? Really?" She walked over to the window and peered out.

Mitchell clenched his jaw. He couldn't go back out into the rain. "Listen, I'll pay you."

"Hey, there's an idea," Penny said, glancing over at Charlie who was shaking her head.

"I couldn't ask you to do that."

"How does a thousand dollars a night sound?" He was getting desperate and needed a shower something terrible. The constant drizzle outside wasn't cutting it.

"A—thou—" Charlie's mouth dropped open.

"Two thousand?"

Her face paled at the words. "I don't think—"

"Three—" he continued, but she raised her hand.

"A thousand is fine." She gave him a weak smile.

Grabbing the handle of his suitcase, he grinned. "Great. Now, which room is mine?"

As if still in a daze, Charlie stumbled from the window. "I'll show you," she said.

When she passed by him, she waved at him to follow. Out in the hall, she led him over to the stairs. When they reached the top, she walked down the hall to the far end.

She stopped outside of a room and waited for him to join her.

"It's not much," she said as she opened up the door and entered. "But it should work."

"That's okay." He followed after her. The room was tiny. It looked as if it could have fit inside of his bathroom at home. Everything was covered in pink wallpaper. A twin bed hugged the far wall with an armoire and dresser crowding the rest of the room.

"This is fine," he said. He'd make this work even though he was used to high thread count sheets and modern amenities.

Charlie walked over to the armoire and opened it. She pulled out a blanket and made her way over to the bed and shook it out. It floated down onto the lumpy mattress.

"There's only one bathroom, I'm sorry to say. It's in the middle of the hall, right across from the stairway."

Mitchell glanced to the door and nodded.

"You'll have to turn the hot all the way to the left. If you don't, the shower won't ever get warm. Also, jiggle the toilet handle or it will run all night. Besides Rose, there are five other residents." She stopped tucking the corners of the blanket and turned to smile at him. "But they go to bed pretty early so don't worry about sharing. Once eight o'clock rolls around, you should have it to yourself."

Mitchell nodded. "Do you stay here?"

Charlie's cheeks flushed. "Yes. I'm downstairs in my grandmother's room."

"You grew up here?"

She nodded. "My parents died when I was five. I've lived here ever since."

Mitchell glanced around. What a strange place to grow up in.

"It wasn't like that. I loved growing up here." Her features softened as she glanced around.

Mitchell could only nod. He understood what it was like to have a special relationship with a grandparent. Too bad his lay in a bed a few doors down and didn't recognize him. "Does she talk about me?"

Charlie looked confused. "Who? Rose?"

Mitchell cleared his throat. "Yeah."

"Some."

"Hmm." He wondered for a moment just what she'd said. How much did this Charlie person know about him?

She brushed the blanket flat and turned. "Bed's ready. I'm gonna head downstairs and get started on dinner. Feel free to make yourself at home."

Mitchell moved past the door so Charlie could slip out. Once she was gone, he shut the door and stared at the room. What a different life this was from his. Even though it looked like the decorations hadn't changed in years, there was a homey feel. One that he was missing in his penthouse in New York.

He grabbed his suitcase and flopped it on the bed. Unzipping it, he found his sweats and Yale t-shirt and headed out into the hallway. A shower sounded amazing.

The bathroom was small, and it was carpeted. He grimaced as he slipped off his shoes. Besides that, the only other thing that he noticed was the fact that there was no lid on the toilet. He leaned over and turned on the shower. Steam billowed over the top of the curtain and filled the room.

He placed his sweats on the toilet tank. Slipping off his suit coat, he inspected it. Yep, just as he thought, it was ruined. He undressed, allowing his clothes to crumple to the ground. They were headed to the garbage anyways.

The water surrounded him as he stepped into the shower. Pressing his hands onto the wall in front of him, he let the water beat on his back. All the stress and worry from the day flowed from his muscles and down the drain.

Pushing off the wall, he grabbed the nearest bottle of soap and lathered up. It wasn't the fancy soap that Sondra, his assistant, bought him, but he felt refreshed as it washed from his body.

Now clean, he shut off the water and reached out for a towel. He located one right above the toilet tank. He grabbed it and dried off.

Wrapping it around his waist, he opened the curtain and cursed. Somehow, while grabbing for a towel, he'd managed to knock his fresh clothes into the toilet. He scrubbed his face with his hands as he glanced around. His room wasn't that far.

After shoving his discarded suit into the trash, he pulled open the door.

"Geez," he exclaimed. Standing in front of him with a shocked expression was Charlie. Her hand was raised as if she'd been interrupted mid-knock.

Her gaze dropped to his chest and then back up. A smiled twitched on his lips as a blush burned on her cheeks.

She raised her hand to shield her gaze. "I'm so sorry. I just wanted to let you know that dinner's ready."

With her eyes covered, Mitchell allowed his gaze to drop to her lips. Her pink, pouty lips. "I knocked my clothes into the toilet," he said.

She pulled her hand down, but kept her gaze focused on the bathroom. "Yeah, sorry about that. I had to remove the lid. Francis kept hiding things in it."

"Francis?"

Her gaze flitted over to him. "Another resident here."

"Was she the one on porch earlier?" The memory of the woman sitting alone entered his mind. He'd felt so helpless when she thought he was someone else.

Charlie nodded. "Yes."

He folded his arms over his bare chest and nodded. "Well, I should probably go get dressed for dinner."

"Yeah. I'll grab a bag and fish out your clothes."

Mitchell reached out, and brushed her arm. "I'll do it."

Her gaze dropped to his hand. "Th-that's okay. I've got it."

"You sure?" he asked.

"Do it all the time. I kind of have a system."

He pulled his hand from her arm and dropped it to his side. Flexing his fingers, he tried to forget the feeling of her soft skin against his. "Thanks."

She nodded. "I'll throw them in the wash as well. They'll be ready after dinner."

"Thankfully, I have a spare," he called out as he headed down the hall to his room. Once inside, he shut the door and dressed. His hand still tingled from their encounter. He rubbed it on his sweats. Nothing he did could remove the memory of her warm skin.

Why was he being so ridiculous? There was nothing between them. If anything, their relationship was a ruse for a woman who couldn't even remember who he was. He towel dried his hair a bit rougher than normal. Anything to get his mind off of Charlie. That's not why he was here. He was here to say goodbye. He needed to remember that.

A chime sounded on the other side of the room. He walked over and picked up his phone. He'd managed to miss fifteen texts from Victoria. Each one more urgent then the next. He half-heartedly scrolled through them. Something about his mother and the business.

His fingers rested on the screen as he read the last message.

I'm coming

5

CHARLIE

*S*he'd seen his chest. His tan, muscular chest. Heat burned her cheeks as she entered the bathroom, thankful for the distraction. As she pulled out a plastic bag that she had stashed under the sink, she focused on the drowning clothing. Nothing cut through romantic thoughts like toilet water.

After she fished out his clothes, she shoved them into the bag and tied it closed. She would go get Rose, then bring the bag downstairs and throw the clothes into the washer.

With her hands sanitized, she shut the bathroom door, and headed down the hall. Two soft knocks on Rose's door, and she waited. There was no response, so she turned the handle and entered.

"Hello?" she whispered as she stepped inside.

Rose hadn't moved from her bed. That wasn't unusual. Rose spent most days tucked under her covers, reading. Sometimes, the same book over and over. A sign that her memory was getting worse.

"Rose?" Charlie approached the bed.

Rose's head tipped to the side, and the sound of her shallow breathing filled the air.

Any other time, Charlie would have just let her sleep. But this afternoon, Rose had only picked at her lunch. If Charlie didn't get Rose's weight up, she might be taken from the house. And that was a thought that Charlie couldn't fathom. She was already dealing with so much loss as it was.

Walking over to her, Charlie reached out and touched her shoulder. "Rose," she said, giving her a little shake.

Rose moaned, but didn't wake.

"Come on, it's time for dinner." Charlie shook her shoulder harder this time.

Rose moaned again, but this time, her eyes fluttered open. "What?" she asked as she righted her head and glanced around. When her gaze fell on Charlie's face, the same confused look rested in her eyes. "Who are you?"

Swallowing against the lump in her throat, Charlie smiled. "I'm Charlie."

Rose's eyes were vacant. "Charlie? Do I know you?"

Charlie pinched her lips together and nodded. "Yes, you do," she whispered.

"Is Tyler here?" Rose asked as her gaze roamed the room.

"Yes."

A smile spread across Rose's lips. "Where?"

"Downstairs. It's time for dinner. He's here to eat with you." Charlie pulled one corner of the comforter back and extended her arm.

The thought of her son seemed to have healing effects on Rose. She swung her legs over the side of the bed and stood. "I'm so excited. It's been too long." She accepted the robe that Charlie handed her and tied it around her waist. "I knew he'd come. I just knew it."

With slippers on, Charlie helped her to the door and out into the hallway.

As they made their way toward the stairs, Floyd's door opened. He glanced at Rose, and then to Charlie.

"How's she this evening?" he asked, his voice full of hope.

All Charlie could do was shake her head. "Not good," she whispered.

His face fell. "Should I come to dinner?"

Charlie shrugged. "If you want."

Rose and Floyd had been together for five years, but now, Rose had no idea who he was. It broke Charlie's heart every time she had to tell Floyd that nothing had changed. He was still a stranger to the woman he loved.

He nodded and slipped into the hallway, shutting his door behind him.

"Do I know you?" Rose asked as Floyd neared them.

"Yes, I'm Floyd," he said as he took her other arm and the three of them headed down the stairs.

Mitchell was sitting at the table as they entered. His hair was still damp, and he was wearing a t-shirt and sweats. Charlie tried hard not to stare, but it was hard when he looked so good unkempt. Why he wore suits boggled her mind.

"Tyler!" Rose exclaimed when she spotted him. "You came." A tear slipped down her cheek as she quickened her pace to reach him.

"Rose, slow down." Charlie smiled as she helped her over. It felt so good to see her so excited.

"Gran—I mean, Rose," Mitchell said as he stood and pulled her into a hug. The embrace lasted longer than a hug between strangers. It made Charlie wonder just what had happened in that family.

Mitchell was the one to break the hug. He helped Rose settle in on her chair and then sat next to her. The casserole that Charlie had made was in the center of the table, and it was no longer steaming.

Charlie pulled out the chair across from Mitchell which allowed Floyd to sit opposite Rose. Once the food was dished up, Floyd and Rose began talking about the current events. It sounded good to hear Rose happy. Charlie blinked, hoping the threatening tears wouldn't fall.

"Thanks," Mitchell said as he leaned forward.

Her gaze fell to him. "What?" she asked.

"Thanks for saving me back there," he said with a half-smile. "You know, with the clothes."

And your naked chest. Charlie's cheeks burned as she shook her head. That was *not* what she should be thinking about. Then she realized that she'd forgotten his clothes outside of the bathroom.

"Shoot. Hang on, I'll be right back." She pushed away from the table and rushed up the stairs.

After starting a load in the basement, she walked into the foyer just in time to see Floyd leading Rose up the stairs. He had her dinner plate in his hand.

"Everything okay?" Charlie asked.

Floyd shook his head. "She was getting tired. Don't worry, I'll make sure she eats more."

Charlie nodded. Once they disappeared at the top of the stairs, she turned her attention back to the kitchen. Back to Mitchell.

He was still sitting at the table when she entered. His gaze met hers, and her breath caught in her throat. He looked sad.

"You okay?" she asked as she headed over to her chair.

He pushed the food around on his plate. "Yeah." He took another bite, and they sat in silence.

"How do you do it?" Mitchell asked.

Charlie glanced over at him. "Do what?"

"Live like this. Day in and day out. Being with someone who doesn't know who you are." He turned his gaze to the table where he pushed some abandoned salt around with his finger.

Charlie swallowed. "It's hard. Living and hoping for those fleeting moments when they remember you." Her stomach twisted as a tear rolled down her cheek. Today's events had been too much. She could no longer keep her emotions at bay.

Feeling stupid, she reached up and wiped the tear from her

face. "I'm sorry," she said. She wasn't hungry anymore, so she grabbed her plate and threw the leftover food into the garbage. At the sink, she flipped on the water and channeled all her frustration into scrubbing the food off.

Chair legs scraped against the floor. "I'm sorry," he whispered from behind her.

A shiver ran down her spine. She could feel his presence. She wanted to turn, but feared his closeness.

He reached out, brushing his arm against hers. "Do you mind if I..." he nodded toward the sink with his plate in hand.

"Sure." She backed away, grateful for the distance that put between them. She'd hadn't felt like this since Alex, and it scared her.

He busied himself with rinsing his plate while she leaned against the far counter, gnawing on her nail. No longer able to stand the silence, she decided to speak up. "So what's your story?"

His half smile returned as he glanced over at her. "My story?"

She tucked a piece of her hair that had fallen out behind her ear. "Yeah. Like, where are you from? What do you do? That sort of thing."

He shut off the water and shook the droplets off his plate. After setting it in the drying rack, he turned. "Well, I'm from New York, and I'm a business man."

"What type of business?"

Grabbing a dish rag, he dried his hands. "Real estate."

"You're a realtor?"

He smiled. "Something like that."

Needing something to do, Charlie walked over to the table, grabbed the casserole, and brought it over to the counter. Francis only ate in her room, so Charlie dished up her plate. Then she wrapped up the rest and put it in the fridge. The other residents ate at different times so would dish up as they wanted.

"How about you?" Mitchell asked.

"Me?"

He nodded.

"My grandmother, Dottie, took care of me."

He glanced around. "She started this place?"

Charlie smiled. "She was an awesome woman. She and Rose were best friends."

A hurt look flashed over his face.

Instantly, Charlie felt stupid. "I'm sorry." Then curiosity got the better of her. "What happened?"

He looked at her with his lips drawn together.

"I'm sorry. You don't have to tell me. It's none of my business." Why did she have to be such an idiot sometimes?

"It's okay. It's just something I don't really like talking about."

Charlie smiled. "It's okay. I get it." For as long as she'd known Rose, Rose never talked about it either.

"Ever been to the states?" he asked.

She shrugged. A few times, but she never liked it. There was something comforting about the expansiveness of Alaska. "A few times."

He gave her a small smile. "Wasn't that impressed with it?"

She shook her head. "Not really."

"This place is that amazing, huh?"

A smile twitched on her lips. "You don't think so?"

Wrinkling his nose, he shook his head. "Not really."

"Well, I think we need to remedy that."

"Oh, really? And how are we going to do that?" His eyebrows shot up.

Charlie chewed her bottom lip. "Come with me tomorrow, and I'll show you."

He paused as he studied her. "It's a date."

That blasted half-smile was back and as much as she didn't want to admit it, heat raced to her cheeks. She grabbed Francis's plate and turned. "I gotta go bring this to a resident."

He nodded, and she slipped from the room. Once she was out of his presence, she felt like she could breathe again. As she climbed the stairs, she shook her head. Why was she so ridiculous sometimes? Falling for the handsome and intriguing stranger? Isn't that what had gotten her into trouble before?

She stood outside of Francis's room and knocked on the door. When no one answered, she headed into the room anyway. After a quick scan, her stomach sank. Francis was gone. Again.

Setting the plate on her dresser, Charlie rushed from her room and out to the hall. After knocking on every door, she began to panic. No one knew where Francis was. She raced down the stairs and into the kitchen where Mitchell stood against the sink, drinking a glass of water.

His watched her with wide eyes. "You okay?"

Charlie shook her head as she pulled open the pantry door and peered inside. Francis wasn't in there. "A resident's missing."

He set the glass down on the counter. "Missing? Who?"

"Francis. She wasn't in her room."

In two steps, he was standing next to her. "Does this happen a lot?"

Charlie nodded. "She gets confused." She made her way over to the back door and grabbed her coat. The image of that small woman lost on the streets of Sitka crowded her mind. "Penny!" Charlie called down the hall.

Penny opened her door. "Yeah?"

"Francis is gone. I'm gonna go look for her. Hold down the fort, okay?"

"Yep," Penny called back.

Charlie turned back to the door and reached for the handle.

"Let me get my shoes. I'll help," Mitchell said.

She glanced down at his hand that he'd wrapped around her arm to stop her. Not sure what to say, she just nodded.

He smiled and removed his grasp. Once she was alone, Charlie took a deep breath. She needed to calm down. Thankfully, this was a small town, and if someone discovered Francis roaming the streets, they would most likely bring her back. There were a few places Francis was most likely to go, but if she wasn't there, Charlie wasn't sure what she'd do.

Needing to do something, Charlie began to button her raincoat. Just as she fastened the last one, Mitchell returned wearing a Yale sweatshirt and shoes.

"Alumni?" she asked, nodding toward the bulldog.

"Yeah."

Charlie raised her eyebrows. Rose had mentioned something about her son marrying a wealthy woman.

Twirling his key ring around his finger, Mitchell pulled open the back door. "Ready?"

Charlie nodded and followed him outside.

The sun had dipped below the trees, but its glow still illuminated the sky. It would light the way.

She couldn't help but notice Mitchell's furrowed brow. His gaze hadn't left her face. He shot her a smile as he made his way over to a pink VW Bug.

"Your chariot, m'lady," he said, dipping down into a bow.

She couldn't help, but smile. Seriously? This was his car?

As if sensing her question, he glanced over at her. "It was the only one left to rent."

"It looks like bubble gum," she said.

He patted the roof of the car. "Yeah. Not something I normally go for."

"I think it's a great color." When she heard the click of the locks releasing, she pulled open the door and slipped onto the seat.

Mitchell started up the engine. "Where to?"

"She doesn't normally go far. Let's keep to the streets around here. There are a few places we can check."

He nodded and pulled onto the main road.

Charlie could walk these streets blindfolded. As she peered out the window, she kept her eyes open for any sign of Francis. Guilt filled her chest. Why couldn't she keep these women safe? It was the last thing she promised her grandmother before she passed away. But right now, she was failing them.

6

MITCHELL

*M*itchell drove the narrow streets according to Charlie's directions. He could tell she was nervous. He wished he could say something to ease her mind, but the words didn't come. The standard sentiments seemed a bit too bland. It took a brave person to take care of the retirement home.

He leaned over and turned on the radio. A soft ballad filled the car. From the corner of his eye, he saw Charlie begin to tap her fingers on her leg.

"Are you a dancer?"

She twisted to look at him. "What?"

"A dancer. You were dancing in the kitchen earlier and now..." He nodded toward her hand.

Her cheeks flushed as she glanced toward his gesture. "Once. Now, I'm too busy." She waved at him to take a left.

He turned on his blinker. "Were you good?"

"I think so."

"Hmm, you'll have to show me sometime. My mom insisted that I learn ballroom dance as a child."

She studied him. "Really? You dance?"

"A bit."

"I can't wait to see it." She turned her gaze outside.

"Don't get your hopes up. It's not that amazing."

Trees surrounded the road as Mitchell drove deeper into the woods. He kept his eyes open for the woman's frizzy hair, but all he saw were branches and leaves.

"Are you sure she'd come here?" he asked.

Charlie nodded. "Yes. It's one of the places."

A few miles down the road the trees stopped. A field had been cleared and gravestones rose up from the grass.

"Stop," she said, raising her hand.

Mitchell pulled off the road.

Charlie opened the door and got out. He followed her. Tucked in the corner of the graveyard was Francis. Her arms were folded as she stared down at a headstone.

"She comes here, you know, when her memory returns," Charlie said as she weaved in and out of the other stones.

"Does it happen a lot?" Mitchell asked as he kept up with her.

"It's happening less and less."

He knew little about the disease. Any words he thought to say seemed superficial.

"Francis?" Charlie said as she approached.

Francis turned. Her eyes were red from tears. "Charlie?" she choked out.

Charlie walked over and pulled Francis into a hug. "You okay?" she asked.

Francis shook her head. "It's been a while since I've been here, hasn't it? The flowers have died." She waved to the pots on either side. Sticks stood up where the flowers once were.

"Almost three months," Charlie said.

"Three months," Francis repeated as she turned her gaze back to the stone.

Neil James Born 1946 Died 2009 Beloved Father and Fisherman was written across the front.

"Was this your husband?" Mitchell asked as he stood next to her.

Francis glanced over at him. "It was."

"What'd he fish for?"

"Everything in the sea. He was stubborn. Always the last one to get out of the water when the season ended."

Mitchell shot her a smile. "Sounds like my kind of guy."

Francis laughed. "He was a character." She peered over at Charlie. "Who's this? Your boyfriend?"

Charlie sputtered and shook her head.

"I'm Mitchell, Rose's grandson." He reached out his hand, and Francis took it.

"It's nice that you came to see Rose. She's really missed you, ya know," Francis said.

His stomach twisted at those words. Had Rose told them about their past? "Yeah?"

Francis nodded. "She was so proud of you and the man you'd become."

Mitchell cleared his throat. Too many emotions had settled there. He didn't know how to process the words Francis had just said. Especially when he doubted their truth.

"Do you have a girlfriend?" Francis's question pulled him from his thoughts.

"What?"

"A girlfriend. Do you have one?" She smiled at him.

After taking a quick peek at Charlie who was focused on tapping a stick with her toe, he turned back to Francis. "Sort of."

Francis walked over to the gravestone and brushed a few leaves off the top. "What does *sort of* mean?"

"I do, but we're not that serious." Why couldn't he just say yes? His gaze found its way back over to Charlie. She had picked the stick up and was pulling bark from it as if to distract herself. He couldn't deny the sparks that had flown between them. If he was honest with himself, he didn't want to be tied down right now.

The girl with the dark hair in front of him might be one of the reasons why.

"Charlie's single," Francis continued. "I mean, she was single." She glanced over to Charlie. "Are you still single?"

Her cheeks reddened. "Francis!" Then her gaze flicked over to him. "Yes, I'm single."

Francis patted Mitchell's arm. "See, she's single."

Mitchell nodded. For some reason, his heart skipped a beat when he heard that.

"If you decided to dump your sort of girlfriend, you should ask Charlie out. You won't find a sweeter or kinder girl anywhere."

"Francis!" Charlie's eyes widened.

Mitchell smiled at Francis. "I promise," he said. He'd be lying if he said he hadn't thought about it.

Francis pulled her sweater tighter around her chest. The rain had started up again. Her face relaxed as she glanced over to Charlie. "Take me home?" she asked.

"Of course," Charlie said, taking her arm and leading her toward his rental car.

Mitchell followed behind as the two women talked softly about the daisies Francis wanted planted in the pots. She insisted that Charlie do it just in case she didn't remember.

Mitchell opened the back door, and helped Francis get in. Charlie climbed into the seat next to her. They continued talking as Mitchell got behind the wheel and started the car.

Once they were back at the retirement home, he helped Francis out of the car and up the back steps. When they got inside, Charlie smiled at him as she took Francis's arm.

"Come on, I'll help you to bed," she said.

Francis nodded, and Mitchell watched as they made their way through the kitchen.

Once they were gone, he took out his phone. He tapped on his text messages and read the last one. *I'm coming.* By the time he'd called Sondra to get her to stop Victoria, Sondra informed him that Vic had already left. Since the flight was roughly eight hours, he'd been unable to reach her on her phone.

Normally, he was used to Victoria intruding in on his life, but right now, the thought angered him. He focused on the door that Charlie had slipped through. He wasn't sure he was ready to share this place just yet.

As if sensing his thoughts, Charlie emerged from the hall. Her shoulders were slumped, and the sparkle in her eye that he'd seen when she was dancing earlier was gone.

"She okay?" he asked.

Charlie glanced over at him and nodded. "She's sleeping now." She sighed as she sat. "Too bad tomorrow she won't remember me and this will start all over again."

He wanted to fix this. How could he make her happy? There was a deep-down need to see her smile. He felt ridiculous for feeling this way. He'd only just met the woman. But the desire was there. And it was eating at him.

Standing, he made his way over to the radio and turned it on. He could feel Charlie's gaze on his back as he flipped through the stations. Finally, he found a slow ballad. Taking a deep breath and feeling like a complete idiot, he turned and headed straight toward her.

Her eyebrows shot up as he reached out his hand.

"Dance with me?" His voice came out lower than he intended.

"Wha—"

He grabbed her hand. Instantly, her gaze dropped to his fingers.

"You do so much for these ladies, it's time you did something for yourself. You said you love dancing. Dance with me."

A look of uncertainty passed over her face. For a second, he thought he'd made a mistake. But she stood, causing his thundering heartbeat to slow to a gallop.

She placed her hand on his shoulder. He wrapped his hand around her waist and pulled her close. Now inches away, he counted the beats in his head, thankful for the distraction that brought him. His mind was screaming from how near she was to him.

He took a step forward, and Charlie stepped back. It only took a few beats until they were waltzing in sync around the kitchen. He could smell the peach scent of her shampoo as he leaned in closer. Her warmth cascaded over him as he tightened his hand on her waist. He never wanted this moment to end.

He applied a little pressure to her hip, indicating he wanted her to spin. She dropped her hand in compliance, and he spun her out.

As she stretched out from him, her gaze met his. That familiar twinkle in her eyes had returned.

"You're not that bad." she giggled as she spun back into his arms.

He reached out and grabbed her hand, pulling her back closer to him. "You're not too bad either," he said into her ear that was inches away.

She turned around and placed her hand onto his shoulder. There was something in her countenance that had changed. She pulled her gaze up to meet his. It held a longing there that he hadn't seen before.

Suddenly, he didn't want the distraction that dancing brought. Instead, he wanted to stand there, lost in her gaze. He dropped her hand, but kept his other one wrapped around her waist. She didn't resist when he brought his now free hand to the other side and pulled her closer.

Her gaze never left his face as she chewed her bottom lip. For a moment, he wondered what her lips might feel like. He leaned down, hoping that she might move to meet him. She tilted her head up, bringing their lips closer together. He hovered there, praying that he was reading her signals right.

"Mitchell, I..." Charlie's voice fell to a whisper. She leaned in for a second, then pulled away. "I'm sorry."

"Mitchell!" A familiar voice reverberated in his ears.

Glancing to the door, he silently cursed. Victoria was standing there with a large, floppy hat and a pink sundress that matched his rental car. Her lips were parted as she glanced between the two of them.

She grabbed the handle of her suitcase and rolled it into the room. "What-what's going on here?" Reaching out, she grabbed his arm and sidled up next to him.

Charlie had backed away and was now staring at the two of them. "I'm sorry. I'm Charlie, and you are?"

Victoria moved closer. "I'm Victoria, Mitchell's girlfriend. Well, who are we kidding? I'm basically his fiancée."

"Fiancée?" Charlie seemed to choke on the word as she glanced over to him.

Mitchell tried to push Victoria away. She didn't budge. "She's my girlfriend. Not my fiancée."

Victoria's high pitched laugh bounced off the walls. "We have a date set, sweetheart."

Mitchell stared at her. "No we don't." From the corner of his eye, he saw Charlie moving toward the door. His gaze whipped to her. "No we don't." He shook his head to emphasize just how much they didn't have a date set. But the look on Charlie's face said she wasn't convinced.

"It's late. You two obviously have a lot to catch up on. I'm just gonna head to bed." She wrapped her arms around her chest as if to protect herself.

"Charlie—" Mitchell stepped toward her.

But she raised her hand. "It's been a long day. I just want to go to sleep." The look in her eye told him not to push it further. But how could he show her that the dance and the almost kiss had meant something to him?

Victoria's fingers encircled his arm, and she pulled him back to her. "I'm here now. I had to finagle the address from Sondra and take a disgusting cab to get here. Let the woman sleep, silly."

He took one last look at Charlie as she slipped from the room and disappeared.

Anger raced through his body as he turned and glared at Victoria. "What are you doing here?"

Victoria batted her eyes at him. Why women did that and thought it was sexy confused him. All it did was make them look like they had something in their eye.

"I missed you. Besides, your mom's freaking out about you not being there to help. So, I promised her that I'd come here and bring you home before you did something you might regret. Looks like I got here right in time." Her gaze turned icy as she glanced up at him.

Mitchell pulled his arm away from her. "But I specifically told you not to come."

The same grating laugh filled the kitchen. "I know. But I thought that was you just doing that thing you do where you say you don't want me, but secretly you do."

He stared at her. Was she serious? He shook his head. It hurt. He needed to get some sleep. This day had been a rollercoaster of emotions. He needed a good night's rest and maybe a drink. "I'm going to bed."

"Great! I'll come with you," she said. The sound of wheels rolling across the tiled floor followed her words.

Mitchel grumbled, but didn't say anything as he led her up the stairs. Hopefully the accommodations would help change her mind. When he opened his bedroom door, Victoria's shoulders tightened.

"This is where you are sleeping?" Distain dripped from her words.

"Yeah, isn't it nice?"

She scoffed as her gaze roamed the room. "It's like pink and tiny. Are you even going to be able to fit on that bed?"

"Yep, because I'll be alone." He gave her a pointed look.

She shook her head. "I don't sleep on anything smaller than a king size bed."

He sat down on the lumpy mattress. "Well, you're going to have to get back on your plane and fly somewhere else. This is the only place that has a vacancy."

"What?"

Sighing, he stood. "I'll go see if Charlie can make you up a bed."

Grateful for a reason to see Charlie and leave Victoria, Mitchell slipped from his room. He breathed a sigh of relief when Victoria didn't follow him. Right now, he wanted to see Charlie again without Victoria hovering over them.

His head pounded as he descended the steps. What would he say to her? As much as he tried to stop them, his thoughts kept returning to her lips.

On the first floor, he peered down the hall. Besides the kitchen and library, there were only two other rooms, and they had their doors shut. One of them had to be Charlie's. Taking a guess, he reached his hand up and knocked.

7

CHARLIE

*S*itting on the chair in front of her vanity, Charlie ran a brush methodically through her hair. She tried to keep her thoughts from falling back to Mitchell and their almost kiss. But she was unsuccessful. She touched her lips as she remembered how close they had gotten.

Sighing, she put the brush down. She could be such an idiot sometimes. Thankfully, she had stopped the kiss. He had a fiancée.

Three knocks pulled her from her thoughts.

She made her way over to the door and opened it.

"Mitchell," she said, her heart quickening.

He was leaning with one arm against the door frame. Maybe it was her eyes, but she swore she saw his face light up when his gaze met hers.

"Sorry to bother you, but I was wondering if you had a room for Victoria."

Pulling her robe over her pj's, she glanced out to the hall. "Is everything okay?"

He nodded. "Yeah. It's just that with her in my room it's a little crowded."

"Oh."

He studied her. "Hey, I wanted to apologize, for earlier. If I overstepped, I didn't mean to. You know, with the dance and the..." his gaze fell to her lips.

"It's okay. We got caught up in the moment. Had I known you were that serious with Victoria, I would've never let it go that far." She shoved her hands into the pockets of her robe and tried to brush away the memory. They had a moment, but she needed to move on. He was spoken for.

His brows furrowed, and he opened his mouth to say something. Instead of allowing this conversation to move into unknown territory, Charlie pushed out to the hall. "I've got a room for her."

She could feel Mitchell as he followed close behind her. Maybe too close. She fought the urge to turn around. She needed to start distancing herself from him. So, she took the stairs two at a time. Just as she neared the top, she tripped.

Hands instantly wrapped around her waist. Mitchell had caught her.

"Whoa, you okay?" he asked.

She straightened, cursing the heat that burned her cheeks from his touch. Instead, she climbed the remaining steps, effectively removing his grasp. "Yep." Pinching her lips together, she headed down the hall. Victoria was standing in the middle of his room, a disgusted look on her face.

"Looking for a room?" Charlie asked, waving her out to meet her.

"If this is the only place, then yes." Victorian's nose crinkled as she joined Charlie.

"It's not fancy, but it's a warm place to sleep." Charlie headed down the hall to the only other vacant room on the floor. She pushed open the door and motioned for Victoria to enter. Victoria's expression remained the same.

Once Charlie made the bed and fluffed the pillows, she gave Victoria the run down on the bathroom, then left, shutting the door behind her. Mitchell remained close. Why was he following her?

She turned to head down the stairs, but he caught hold of her elbow.

"Hey."

She pulled away, and he glanced over at her, one eyebrow raised. She rubbed her arm. "What's up?"

"I want to pay you, you know, for Victoria's room."

She glanced around. Did he figure it out? Did he know she was broke? "It's okay. Don't worry about it. I'm happy to have her." That was a lie.

He reached out, but she backed away. They really needed to stop touching.

"Please, let me do this. I won't take no for an answer," he said.

She wanted to keep rejecting him, but the truth was, she needed the money. "Okay, if you insist."

A half-smile spread across his lips. "Thanks."

She nodded and started down the stairs.

"I'll see you tomorrow?" he asked.

"I have nowhere else to go." She glanced up at him.

"Can't wait to see what makes this island so great."

She shot him a small smile then bounded down the rest of the steps. Inside her room, she crawled under her covers and pulled them up over her head. Hopefully tomorrow she'd feel better. Tomorrow, these feelings better disappear.

Charlie's alarm buzzed way too soon. It felt as if she'd just fallen asleep. But breakfast wouldn't cook itself. Pulling off her covers, she rubbed her face and pulled open the door. A shower. She needed one badly.

Once she was clean, she slipped out of the bathroom. Back in her room, she dressed. Pulling her hair up in to a bun, she opened her door and made her way to the kitchen.

Just as she entered, she stopped. Mitchell was standing in front of the counter, looking confused.

She took a deep breath. "Good morning," she said, walking up to him.

He turned, flashing her that half smile again. "Morning."

She grabbed the coffee maker from the cupboard and set it on the counter.

"Ah, that's where that was. I'm in desperate need."

"I'd say. You're up early."

"Actually, it's eleven o'clock in New York." He began searching the cupboards, but stopped once he'd found the mugs. "Want one?"

She nodded and started the coffee maker.

They sat at the table while they waited for it to finish.

Charlie tried to keep her gaze from his face, but she was unsuccessful. Especially when he was smiling like that.

"Did you sleep well?" She prayed making conversation would help distract her.

He shrugged. "Wasn't a five-star hotel, but it wasn't bad. I did struggle with how bright it was."

"Yeah. You gotta get used to that here."

He smiled at her again.

"And Victoria? Is she up yet?" She needed to remind herself that he had a girlfriend.

"Naw, I don't think so. She was never the early riser type."

Charlie traced the wood grain table top with her finger. "How long have you two been together?"

"A year. But her family has been friends with mine since we were teens." He leaned back and rested his hands behind his head.

They had a history. A twinge of pain pounded in Charlie's heart. "That's nice. I've always been a fan of those type of love stories." Gah, why did she sound so dumb? She stood and made her way over to the coffee that was brewing.

"I wouldn't classify what we have as a love story." Thankfully, Mitchell had remained seated at the table.

"Oh?" she said.

"In fact, I've been thinking lately that perhaps we're not—"

"Are you going to introduce her to Rose?" Charlie wasn't sure if she wanted to hear the end of that sentence. She didn't want him to give her false hope.

Mitchell studied her for a moment then shrugged. "Not sure yet."

Once the coffee pot was full, Charlie pulled it out and filled up each mug. "Do you like it black?" She moved over to the table.

Mitchell nodded and took it from her. They sat in silence, each sipping at the steaming liquid.

Penny walked in a few minutes later. She had on a flowy floral dress and a pair of black rimmed glasses. She smiled at Charlie then over to Mitchell. "How'd you sleep?" she asked as she filled up a mug and sat next to Charlie.

Mitchell twisted his head and rolled his shoulders. "It was a bit lumpy, but I slept well."

Charlie's face heated. This was the first time she'd ever been embarrassed by this place. Mitchell seemed to like nice things. No doubt he stayed in places that worried about their amenities and not missing residents. Just another reason why she should push the thoughts of being with him out. He'd never want to stay here and that was all she wanted to do.

A thundering sound came from outside the dining room and drew their attention toward it. It grew louder until Victoria burst through the door. She had green goop on her face, and her hair was pulled up into a messy bun. She didn't even acknowledge anyone as she raced over to the coffee pot and filled a mug.

"Good morning, Victoria," Charlie said as she stood and made her way to the sink and rinsed her cup.

Victoria groaned as she peered at Charlie from over the rim of the mug.

"Sleep well?" Mitchell asked.

"Who's this?" Penny asked, looking over to Mitchell.

"She's my girlfriend who decided to drop in from New York," he said.

The more he said girlfriend, the easier it was for Charlie to hear. It helped put distance between the two of them, and what had almost happened last night.

Victoria lowered the mug and set it on the counter. She pushed her hand into her lower back. "That mattress is awful. You should burn it. No one in their right mind should sleep on it."

"Vic!" Mitchell hissed as he shot Charlie an apologetic look.

"It's okay. I understand. Except, we can't really afford new mattresses here. And on the island, we try to use things until they wear out."

Victoria rolled her shoulders. "Well, from the knots in my back I'd say, it's worn out. Do you have a masseuse here?"

Was she kidding? Charlie just told her that they couldn't afford new mattresses. How would they afford a masseuse? "Naw. Can't afford those either."

"Hmm. Maybe we can find one we when go out today. You are taking me shopping, right?" Her gaze fell to Mitchell who glanced over at Charlie.

"Well, I promised Charlie I'd see parts of the island—"

"It's okay," Charlie said. "You should go out with Victoria. There are lots of fun shops around here." She was grateful that this gave them a reason not to go out today.

He raised an eyebrow. "You sure?"

Charlie pinched her lips together and nodded. "Totally sure. Go with Victoria. Have fun. Besides, I have to head out and find another job."

Mitchell's face fell. "Charlie, I—"

She raised her hand. "It's okay. Really, I'm over it." And that was the truth. There was something about his half-smile and the sweet way he spoke to Francis yesterday that helped push out all the frustration she'd felt from the day before.

Before she delved into the ridiculous fantasies about the two of them, she excused herself to get ready in her room. Victoria had settled in next to Mitchell, and Penny was pulling bacon and eggs out of the fridge to get started on breakfast.

Back in her room. Charlie pulled her hair out of the bun and shook out the waves. She switched her top a few times until she decided to forgo her normal jeans and shirt for a deep blue sundress. From the light that burst into her bedroom, today might actually stay sunny. She welcomed its brightness. It helped lighten her mood. Slipping on a pair of sandals, she pulled open her door.

Once again, Mitchell stood on the other side of it with his hand raised.

She squeaked and jumped back.

He smiled. "Sorry. Didn't mean to scare you."

She leaned against the doorframe hoping she looked casual. "It's okay. Did you knock?"

"No. I was about to."

She pinched her lips together. "Did you need something?"

He pulled out his phone. "I figured that I should get your number in case Victoria gets bored and my afternoon frees up."

She grabbed her purse and stack of resumes from the dresser next to the door and nodded. "Okay." She rattled off her number, and he punched it into his phone.

As he tucked the phone back into his jeans, he turned to her. "Hopefully, she doesn't take a long time."

Charlie pushed past him and shut her door. "It's fine. I was only going to take you to Totem Pole park. But it'll be there tomorrow."

"Totem Pole park, huh? Sounds fun."

"It is." Charlie stopped and turned. "Make sure you see Rose today. Even though she thinks you're your father, you never know what might trigger her memory. And trust me, you'd hate yourself if you missed it." She hated leaving Rose and Francis every day, but this place needed to stay open. She had to risk missing when they remembered every time she stepped from the house.

"I will. I promise." He leaned forward, but Charlie took a step back.

She smiled at him, hoping he didn't notice. "Good." She grabbed her purse strap. "Well, I should go."

He nodded. "I'll call you if my plans change."

Once she was in the car, she placed her purse and resumes on the seat next to her and took a deep breath. She needed to be careful. Relationships never ended well for her, and she couldn't put herself through that kind of heart break again. Especially not when the guy was already spoken for.

8

MITCHELL

*A*fter returning to the kitchen, breakfast dragged on. Mitchell found himself missing Charlie. She wasn't there to brighten up the room.

Victoria chatted about the newest remodel of her New York flat, and Penny tried to feign interest. Thankfully, Victoria didn't notice and seemed content to hear herself talk. Other residents slipped into the kitchen for breakfast and out again. Penny explained that most of them had families or a job around town, so rarely stuck around.

Once Victoria started in on the remodels she had planned for Mitchell's office, Penny excused herself to go check on Francis and Rose. She left the kitchen a little too quickly for someone her age.

When they were finished with breakfast, Mitchell stood and washed both dishes. Victoria remained next to him, inspecting her nails. He should have known she'd never help. Her hands were too delicate—she claimed.

He stacked the dishes in the drying rack and turned. Victoria was messing around on her phone.

"You done?" she asked as she glanced up at him.

"Yep."

"Good. I'll go get ready, and then we can head out."

He wiped his wet hands on his jeans. "While you do that, I'm going to go check on my grandma."

Victoria nodded, and they headed up the stairs. She disappeared into her room, and Mitchell made his way to Rose's door. He stood outside of it and paused, taking a deep breath. Charlie made all of this look so easy. He wished she was here.

He knocked a few times and waited.

"Come in," Rose's small voice called from the other side.

He turned the handle and slipped into the room.

She broke out into a smile. "Tyler," she said, raising her arms and waving him in for a hug.

"Hey, Rose," he said, fighting the urge to call her grandma, and embraced her.

"I'm so happy you've finally come to see me. It's been too long."

He pulled a chair up next to her bed. "It has."

Rose gave him a big smile and reached out her hand. He took it, and she enclosed it with her other hand. "So what's new? Tell me about Mitchell. How's he doing?"

Mitchell swallowed as pain pricked his heart. "He's doing fine. He misses you."

A sad smile spread across her lips. "I miss that boy, too. Is he still playing baseball? He was such a good hitter."

Mitchell scrubbed his face with his free hand. His grandma was such a baseball fanatic, and he hated himself for quitting after she left. "Well, you know kids. If you're not there to make sure they practice they're bound to give it up."

Rose giggled. "That's true." She paused and glanced out the window. "Will you bring him to see me?"

Tears gathered in Mitchell's eyes. Was he ever going to be able to say he was sorry to his grandma? Or was this it? Was he being punished for the past? She glanced back up at him with her eyebrows raised as if she were waiting for an answer. "Sure. I think he'd like that."

She patted his hand then her face grew serious. "How are things with Jocelyn? Is she still upset with me?"

Frustration brewed in his stomach at the mention of his mom. It was easier when it Rose didn't remember her. But today, memories of his mom seemed fresh in her mind.

What should he do? Should he lie? It felt wrong to tell his fragile grandmother that his mom still hated her. When the truth was, his mom should forgive. His brother's death had been an accident.

He engulfed her hand with his other one. "It wasn't your fault."

A tear slipped down Rose's cheek. "But if I had only seen that truck…" her gaze drifted to the window again.

He squeezed her hand. She needed to know that he didn't blame her and it was wrong for his mom to.

Rose turned back and gave him a small smile. "Tell Mitchell that I'm sorry. I didn't mean to leave like that."

He cleared his throat. "I will."

"Mitchell!" Victoria called from down the hall.

Rose looked confused as she glanced around the room. "Is he here?"

Panic set in. "I'll be right back." He jumped from his seat and met Victoria in the hall. "What?" he asked.

She spun to show off her outfit. "I'm ready."

He shook his head. "That's all you wanted to say? I'm talking to my grandma."

Victoria either didn't notice his tone or chose to ignore it as she pushed past him and entered Rose's room. "She's in here?"

"Vic," he said, trailing after her.

Rose was smiling again as she glanced back and forth from the two of them. "Tyler!" she exclaimed as if she were seeing him for the first time today.

Crap. He had to start this all over again.

"You're here!" She opened her arms, and he walked over and gave her a hug. "It's been too long. Who did you bring to see me?"

"This is Victoria." He nodded in her direction.

"His fiancée," Victoria added as she stepped forward.

"Oh, it's so nice to meet you." Rose opened her arms for a hug, but Victoria just stood there, her gaze sweeping over Rose. Mitchell could tell from the disgusted look on her face, she did not want to hug his grandmother.

Frustrated with how she was acting, Mitchell patted Rose's hand then walked over to Victoria. "We should go." He turned to Rose. "I'll be back."

Her face fell, but then she attempted a smile. "Okay. I'll hold you to that."

Mitchell grinned at her. "I'm sure you will."

Rose reached over, grabbed a book from the nightstand, and pulled out her reading glasses. Mitchell motioned to Victoria who seemed a bit too eager to leave as she nearly bounded out the door.

"That was your grandmother? She's so old," Victoria said as Mitchell shut the door.

He gritted his teeth. "That's what a grandmother is, Vic."

She pulled a file from her purse and began filing her nails. "I'm never getting old."

"What?" he said as he followed her down the stairs and outside to his car.

"I mean it," she said.

He shook his head. He was starting to realize how different they both were. He couldn't even remember the reason why he'd started dating her in the first place. Perhaps it was because he felt that it was his responsibility. He needed to keep up appearances. At least that was what his mom had said.

He shook his head. Right now, he couldn't even think about his mom. It angered him how she had left things with Rose. He had half a mind to call her up right now and tell her how he felt.

"Why did she call you Tyler?" Victoria asked as she climbed into his car.

"She thinks I'm my dad."

Victoria groaned. "Now she thinks I'm engaged to your dad?"

Mitchell started his car. "About that, stop telling people we're engaged. We're not." Anger grew in his chest as he remembered the look on Charlie's face when Victoria told her that she was his fiancée.

Victoria's long fingers wrapped around his hand that was resting in his lap. "We both know that's not true. You were going to propose. I saw the ring."

She'd lost her mind. He turned to her. He didn't even know how to respond. "Ring? What ring?"

Victoria rolled her eyes. "The ring you left on your night-stand." She leaned over and rest her head on his shoulder. "The one you left for me to find."

What was she talking about? He'd never bought a ring in his life. "Vic, I didn't buy you a ri—"

"Ooo, a store!" Victoria shot up and pointed toward the shops that lined the road. "Pull over, pull over!"

Still trying to figure out how a ring got on his nightstand, Mitchell complied. Did someone buy a ring and put it next to his bed?

Before he even put the car into park, Victoria had opened her door and was on the sidewalk. He shook his head to clear it and turned off the car. What a weird conversation.

Victoria ran into the fur shop as Mitchell got out. It wasn't abnormal for him to follow after her as she shopped. There were very few things that Victoria did and shopping was one of them. He would pass the time on his phone negotiating large real estate deals.

After grabbing a few coats, Victoria slipped into the dressing rooms. Mitchell found an empty chair and swiped his phone on. Charlie's name appeared. He stared at it. It was strange that he felt such a connection to her in such a short amount of time. This wasn't like him. He was a sensible guy. Very rarely did he jump into anything.

But there was something about her. Her kindness toward Rose and Francis. The way she had told him off after he got her fired. The vulnerability she showed. The way she chewed her lip when she was nervous. All these parts of her intoxicated him and drew him in.

"Hello? Mitchell?" Victoria's whine pushed through his thoughts.

He glanced over to see her standing in front of him with a dark fur coat wrapped around her body. "Hmm?" he asked.

"What do you think?" She took her time twirling around.

He shut off his phone. "It's great, but don't you have like ten already?" He stood and made his way over to the window and glanced outside. He didn't want to be here.

"Yeah, but you can never have too many," she said.

As he stared out to the street and the bustling crowds that swarmed it, he wondered what Charlie was doing at this moment. Had she found another job? His heart sank as he remembered how he'd acted in the diner. She was fired and out searching for a job because of him.

A surge of excitement raced through his body. He could fix this.

"Vic, I'm gonna be right back." He started toward the door but paused. "Here are my keys. Drive back when you're finished." He threw them onto a nearby table.

"But—"

He pushed through the door before she could continue. Quickening his pace, he started down the street, then stopped. Four stores down from the fur shop was a mattress store. Another idea entered into his mind. A smile twitched as he pulled open the mattress store's door.

"Hello, sir. How can I help you today?" the salesman asked as he approached Mitchell.

Glancing around, Mitchell located the twin mattresses. "How many twin mattresses do you have in stock?"

"Here in the store? Why? How many are you looking to buy?"

Mitchell tried to think back to the house. There were four doors on each side of the hall upstairs and two bedrooms downstairs. "Ten?"

The salesman's eyes bugged. "Ten?"

Mitchell nodded.

The salesman walked over to the computer that was in the middle of the room and began typing. "If you're okay with getting four different kinds, then I can scrounge up ten twins."

Mitchell pulled out his wallet and smiled. "Perfect."

After he paid for delivery and removal of the old mattresses, Mitchell left the store and headed down the street toward Jorge's Diner.

He pulled open the door and nearly collided with Charlie's friend.

She gave him a dirty look. "What are you doing back here?"

Mitchell shot her a smile, hoping it might soften her up a bit. It didn't work. She continued her icy stare. He glanced down to her name tag. "Priscilla, right? Is Jorge here?"

"Why? Do you want to get another one of us fired?"

Mitchell furrowed his brow. "No."

She humph as she studied him. Finally, she sighed. "Wait here. I'll go get him."

A few minutes later, a perturbed Jorge pushed through the kitchen door. His gaze fell on Mitchell. "If you're here with a dry-cleaning bill, I'm sorry, but that's not our policy."

Mitchell stared at him. "What?"

"Your suit from yesterday was ruined. I'm sorry, but we don't reimburse for that."

Mitchell shook his head. "No. That's not why I'm here. I

wanted to apologize for how things went yesterday. In fact, I was hoping I could convince you to give Charlie her job back."

Jorge's face reddened as he stared at him. "Give Charlie her job back? Why?"

Priscilla squeaked from where she stood behind Jorge.

"I made a mistake. I wasn't in my right mind yesterday. That whole situation was my fault." He clasped his hands together in front of him.

Jorge studied him. "I'm sorry. That wasn't the only reason why I let her go. She's been late a lot. It's like she doesn't take this job seriously."

This wasn't going well. He needed to do something. Glancing around and taking in the state of the dining room, he got an idea. "What if I were to become an investor? You could use the money to spruce this place up. Maybe get new booths? You know, do a remodel?"

"What?" Jorge looked confused.

"Please? You'd be helping me out." There was no way Charlie would just take money from him. This was the only way to ensure she'd be taken care of. "How does two hundred and fifty thousand sound?" Honestly, he had no idea how much fixing up a restaurant of this size would cost. All he knew was remodeling the real estate he bought at home cost a lot more.

"A-a quarter of a million?" Jorge breathed out.

"What!" Priscilla exclaimed.

Jorge turned and shot her a look. She gave him a small smile and headed over to the table where three kids were throwing french fries at the wall.

Mitchell turned back to Jorge. "Do we have a deal?"

Jorge just stood there with a dazed expression.

"Hello?" Mitchell leaned in.

"Yeah, yeah." Jorge cleared his throat. "I think we have a deal."

Mitchell extended his hand. "Perfect."

9

CHARLIE

*C*harlie slipped onto a booth at Jorge's diner. She was exhausted. It seemed that there was nothing more tiring then waiting for someone who had your number to call. Every beep and every vibration sent her heart galloping. When she would check her phone, and see it wasn't Mitchell, her stomach would sink.

Priscilla walked up to her with her eyes wide and a goofy look on her face. Obviously, she was having a better day than Charlie was.

"What's with you?" she asked when Priscilla slipped onto the booth across from her. "And why are you sitting? Jorge's going to freak when he sees you."

Priscilla pinched her lips shut and shook her head. "Not today. He's walking on cloud nine."

When Charlie located Jorge at the edge of the diner his gaze met hers. He looked giddy as he started making his way toward her.

"Charlie! I'm so glad to see you," he exclaimed as he reached out and grabbed her hand.

"Okay?" she said. What was happening?

"I'm so sorry about what happened yesterday. Please, come back to work."

That was not what she was expecting to hear. "What?"

Jorge laughed. It sounded strange. "Please come back. I'm sorry I fired you. What was it even about anyways?"

"Um, I dumped water in a customer's lap."

He laughed again. Charlie glanced over to Priscilla for answers, but she had the same look on her face.

"It's all forgotten." He waved his hand at his forehead. "So, will you come back?"

This was strange, but it did help her in the money department. "Okay."

Jorge reached out and grasped her hand again. "Thank you." He stood and nearly danced his way over to the cash register.

Charlie turned back to Priscilla. "That was weird, huh?"

Priscilla shook her head. "No. It's not weird."

Charlie had enough of this. Leaning forward, she stared into her best friend's eyes. "What is going on? Why do you both have these ridiculous grins on your faces?"

"You will never believe what happened earlier. Apparently, the guy that got you fired yesterday came in to the restaurant and asked Jorge to give you your job back."

Charlie's brows furrowed. "What?" Mitchell came in here? Why?

"Oh, that's not all. Apparently, he's loaded. He offered Jorge a quarter of a million to take you back."

Charlie nearly choked. "What?"

"Yeah."

"Mitch—I mean the guy came in and offered Jorge money to give me my job back?" Where would he have gotten that kind of cash? Was he lying? It wasn't funny if he was. She was sure if Mitchell didn't pay, Jorge would fire her so fast. She needed to talk to Mitchell. Right now. "Hey, I should go."

"But you just got here."

Charlie stood. "Yeah, but I've been away from the house for a while. I should get back to give Penny a break. I'll see you tomorrow at the festival."

Priscilla nodded, and Charlie sprinted from the diner. Outside, she took in a few deep breaths. Rose had mentioned that her son had married a wealthy woman, but never said how much. Charlie would have never guessed it was "give a quarter of a million away" kind of rich.

She started down the road, and her phone rang. Pulling it from her purse, she hit talk.

"Hello?"

"Charlie?"

His familiar voice excited and angered her at the same time. "Mitchell?"

"Yeah. I was wondering if you wanted meet up. I'm at Totem Pole park right now."

Oh yes, she wanted to meet up. "I'll be there in five." She unlocked her car door and slipped in. The whole drive over she thought about what she was going to say. How does one chew out another person for giving a former boss a ton of money to take them back? The whole situation was strange.

She pulled into the parking lot and got out. She smoothed down her dress and walked into the visitor's center. Mitchell had on a headset and was staring at a carving of a huge frog. She walked up to him and tapped him on the shoulder.

"Charlie," he said as he pulled the headphones from his ears. "It's good to see you." His smile angered her more.

Why was he so good looking? She put on her serious face. Anything to help her stay focused. "Yeah. Can we talk?"

He looked a bit confused, but nodded. "Sure."

She pushed through the doors and stepped outside. They started down the path that led through the park. A totem pole rose up from the ground in front of her. She stomped by it. There was no way she could enjoy this place until she gave him a piece her mind.

As they went deeper down the path, Mitchell followed behind her. Suddenly, she stopped and whipped around. "What the heck, Mitchell?"

He narrowed his eyes. "What?"

"You bribed my former boss to give me my job back?"

His face reddened at her accusation. Crap. It was true.

"You know about that?" he asked.

"Yeah. I went in there and both Jorge and Priscilla were giddy. A quarter—" she lowered her voice and glanced around to make sure no one was listening. "A quarter of a million dollars? Are you crazy? You know what's going to happen to me when you can't make the payment, don't you? He'll fire me and then what was the point?"

Mitchell stared at the totem pole in front of them. "What do you mean, when I don't pay him?"

She took a step back. "You're saying you have a quarter of a million to just give away?"

His gaze met hers. "Yes. I'm his investor now."

There was a look in his eye that told her he was serious. "What are you like a multi-millionaire?" she asked.

He nudged the ground with the tip of his shoe. "More like... billionaire."

There were no words. Charlie opened her mouth, but when nothing came out, she closed it again. Turning, she made her way down the path.

"Hey," Mitchell called from behind her. "Hey." His hand surrounded her elbow.

She stopped. Her spine tingled from his touched. No matter what she was feeling right now, her grandma raised her to be a hard worker. The fact that this man felt like he could come into her life and throw money at her problems bothered her. "Why did you do that?"

"I felt bad. After all, I was the one that got you fired." He glanced over at her. "Besides, I knew you'd never just take my money."

She snorted. "That's right." She studied him. The worst part about all of this was, he looked sincere. "I was going to be okay. I can find a job." She crossed her arms in front of her chest.

He nodded. "I know."

"I didn't need your help or your money."

"I believe you."

She bit her lip as she studied him. Maybe she was overreacting a bit. "Promise you won't do that again? Use your money to do things for me? You owe me nothing."

He raised his right hand. "I promise."

Tucking her hair behind her ear, she gave him a small smile. He returned it, looking relieved.

They stood in silence as Mitchell glanced around.

"This is Totem park?"

Charlie nodded. "Yep."

"It's nice. Though I have to say, I don't know much about them."

She turned and started down the path with Mitchell next to her. "They were carved by a group of Native Americans called the Tlingets. They occupied most of the southwest area of Alaska."

They walked through the park. Charlie gave him information about the tribes and the totem poles, and Mitchell nodded along with it. Once they finished, Charlie turned to him feeling stupid that she yelled at him.

"I'm sorry for overreacting."

He smiled. "I understand. You're a strong, independent woman. I should've asked before I just acted. Maybe you're right. I do throw my money at problems."

She nodded. "But when you have as much as you do, I guess that's what you're used to."

"Yeah. It came with a price though. My parents worked hard to build up their real estate business that they kind of forgot they had kids. That's why my grandma raised me. She stepped in where they fell short." He smiled. "But it was for the best. She taught me to be humble. She insisted we learn about hard work. Where my parents would have just given us whatever we wanted."

Charlie sat down on a nearby bench, and Mitchell joined her. She glanced over at him. It must have been hard to have parents who didn't take the time to spend it with him. Her parents were gone, so couldn't disappoint her.

"I'm sorry," she said

He shrugged. "I got used to it."

She stared off to the ocean that spanned out in front of them. The sun warmed her skin. Taking in a deep breath, she closed her eyes.

"I'm starting to see it."

Looking over at him, she tried to keep her gaze steady. "See what?"

His gaze didn't leave her face. "Why you like this place."

She shivered at the intensity of his stare, so glanced back to the glistening blue water. "It's beautiful, isn't it?"

"It is."

He was still staring at her.

"Charlie?"

That voice. Where did she know it from? Turning, she glanced over her shoulder, and her heart fell. Looking as good as the day she walked out on him was her ex.

"Alex?" She leapt from the bench. Her cheeks burned as she smoothed down her skirt. "What are—what are you doing here?"

Movement next to her drew her attention over. Mitchell had stood and was staring at Alex.

"Just got back." Alex glanced over at Mitchell as he stepped up to her. "Could I talk to you in private?"

Charlie's heart pounded so loud she could barely make out what he was saying. He was back and standing in front of her. Why?

Alex reached out and touched her elbow. "Please?"

Pinching her lips together, Charlie nodded. "Um, yeah, sure." She allowed him to guide her away. With her emotions muddling her brain, she struggled to do the simplest tasks.

When they were out of earshot of Mitchell, Alex stopped and turned. "You look good," he said, flashing her one of his familiar smiles.

Heat raced to her cheeks. "So do you." Ugh, why did she say that? She should be telling him off or smacking him. Not complimenting him on his looks.

His hand remained on her elbow. His fingers warmed her skin. It was all too much. She pulled away before she allowed herself to go down memory lane. "Why'd you come back?"

Alex peered over at her as he grasped his hands in front of him. "I made a mistake, Char. I was stupid. I'm back because I've changed. I want you in my life. You were the best thing that ever happened to me. I was an idiot for hurting you."

She studied him, and her stomach twisted into knots. This was just too much. First, Rose's struggles, then being behind on bills, and now this? Her emotions couldn't take it anymore. Instead of answering him, she turned and walked away.

"Charlie?" Two male voices called after her. She waved her hand at them. Right now, she just needed to be alone.

When she got to her car, she pulled open the door, and slipped inside. With both hands on the wheel, she stared out the windshield. Mitchell and Alex emerged from the visitor's center. They kept glancing at each other. Finally, Mitchell walked up to Alex and shook his hand.

Reaching down, she started the car and peeled out of the parking lot. Both men glanced in her direction as she raced past them.

The more distance she put behind her, the better she felt. The trees and shrubbery rose up around her. That was the benefit of living in a rainforest. It didn't take long before she was surrounded and secluded.

Pulling the car over to the side of the road, Charlie got out. She slammed the door and started walking. Twigs snapped beneath her feet. The smell of impending rain surrounded her. She took in a deep breath, and her muscles began to relax.

The deeper she went into the woods, the clearer her mind became. Why had Alex come back? Was he here to torture her? She reached out and slapped a nearby branch that hung above her. When she'd caught him kissing another girl, she thought her heart would break.

Thankfully, he got a job in the states working for his uncle's construction company. That meant, she would never see him again.

"Ha!" she said, as she pushed a bush aside and continued on. Fat chance. She sat down on a fallen tree trunk and wrapped her arms around her stomach. He should have stayed away. Her heart couldn't take him being back.

Sitting alone and staring into the trees soothed her. All her problems didn't exist here. The weight of the retirement home, Rose and Francis's illness, and the big fat failure her romance life was— didn't matter.

She laid on the tree and stared up at the sky. She'd stay here forever. Closing her eyes, she took a deep breath.

It wasn't until she felt a fat raindrop splash on her forehead that she sat up. Glancing at her watch, she sighed. It was half past six. Penny would be wondering where she was.

Charlie slipped off the tree and started making her way back to her car. Or at least she thought she was. If she was completely honest with herself, she couldn't really remember which way she'd come. Trying to muster all her girl scout abilities, she stared up at the sky. Had she come east or west?

Suddenly, her foot caught on an exposed root and she pitched forward. She reached her hands out to break the fall, but it was too late. Her head smacked against the nearby tree and everything went black.

MITCHELL

*T*he rain was coming down harder now, and Charlie still hadn't returned. Mitchell paced in the front room, staring out the window. Every time a car drove by, he stopped. But when he realized it wasn't Charlie, he continued.

"You're going to wear the carpet out," Penny said as she stepped into the room holding two mugs. "Tea?"

Mitchell shook his head. His stomach was too knotted to put anything in it.

"Don't worry, she'll be back. Sometimes, she just needs a minute to breath."

Mitchel glanced at Penny, trying to take his cue from her. She had known Charlie much longer. If she wasn't worried, why was he? He stared out the window. He knew why. Because Penny hadn't seen the look on Charlie's face when she'd run from Totem park.

Laughter came from the kitchen. Mitchell's ears pricked as he made his way from the room and barreled into Victoria who had an armful of bags.

"Hey," she complained until she saw his face. "What's going on?"

He shook his head. "Sorry." He pulled out a chair and collapsed onto it.

She dropped the bags and sat next to him. "Well, I'm happy I caught you. I was at the jewelry store and found this." Reaching out, she flashed her hand at him. On the fourth finger of her left hand was a one carat diamond.

"What?" He furrowed his brow as he turned to look at her. "Why'd you buy that?"

Victoria pulled the best innocent face. "What do you mean? I figured you were going to ask me, so shouldn't I get the ring I actually want?"

Mitchell scrubbed his face. He didn't want to deal with this now. "Whatever." He'd address this later. Right now, he needed to find Charlie. He stood and made his way to the back door. It was pouring outside.

"Vic, where are my keys?"

She held her hand out, and he grabbed them. Once Charlie was back and safe, he'd confront Victoria about the ring.

Ducking his head, he raced through the rain and out to his car. He started it up and peeled out onto the street.

Fifteen minutes passed and he still hadn't located her. Every siren was going off in his mind. The car's wipers squealed as they swished against the windshield. The rain was pouring so hard that he could barely see the road in front of him.

He took a left and leaned forward, squinting to see through the droplets. A red car was parked along the side of the road. He slowed and rolled the passenger window down. It was Charlie's car. He pulled in front of it and turned off the engine.

His heart pounded as he circled around the abandoned vehicle, peering into the windows. There didn't seem to be anything out of the ordinary. He glanced into the woods. Was it possible? Did she leave her car to go wandering in the woods?

Rain rolled down his back. He was drenched now. He could

only imagine what she looked like. Taking out his phone, he made sure he had a charge and pushed into the woods.

"Charlie?" he called out against the wind that blew through the trees.

Nothing.

"Charlie?" he called louder. He strained to hear her.

Nothing again.

Branches slashed at his arms as he pushed through the woods. She had to be here somewhere.

"Charlie!" he yelled as he scanned his surroundings. A speck of color caught his attention. "Charlie?" He approached it.

His stomach twisted. Charlie was sprawled on the ground. He sprinted to her side and pulled her head into his lap. Her eyes were closed, and she had a huge gash running down her forehead.

"Charlie, can you hear me?" He leaned down to feel if she was breathing. Shoving his fingers onto her throat, he concentrated on her pulse.

She moaned, and his heart soared. "Alex?" she whispered.

That was a punch to the gut. Mitchell shook his head. "It's Mitchell."

She opened her eyes and stared around. "Where's Alex?"

"I don't know. You fell, Charlie. I'm gonna get you out of here." He scooped her up, and pulled her close. She rested her head against his shoulder. "Don't worry, I've got you," he whispered.

The need to protect her raced through his chest as he pushed back the way he'd come. Rain splattered on his face, but he shook it off. Charlie started shivering. He pulled her closer to keep her warm.

Why did she think he was Alex? He swallowed. Secretly, he'd been hoping there had been something between them. He'd thought she'd felt it too. Apparently not.

He burst from the woods and made his way over to his car. Opening the passenger door, he placed her on the seat then rushed around to the driver's side and got in. The engine roared to life, and he fiddled with the temperature until heat burst from the vents.

Charlie was more awake now and glancing around. Her gaze landed on him, and her eyebrows shot up. "Mitchell?"

His grip tightened on the steering wheel. He forced a smile and turned. "Yeah."

"What are you doing? How did I get here?" She straightened in her seat and peered around.

"I came looking for you. You were passed out."

"So… you came and rescued me?"

He nodded.

"Where's Alex?" She sounded confused.

"I'm not sure." His heart tore open at every mention of Alex. Why was this affecting him so much?

"Hmm. I thought he was here." She wrapped her arms around her chest and stared out the window.

"I'm going to take you to the hospital. You should get checked out."

Charlie shook her head. "No. I can't afford that. Just take me home. I have a headache, but I'll be okay."

"Don't worry about it. I can pay—"

"No. No, thank you. I'll be fine. I don't want to owe you."

He glanced over at her. He wanted to tell her that it really was no big deal, but her jaw was set so he dropped it. He'd check on her tonight to make sure she didn't have a concussion. "If that's what you want."

Charlie nodded.

Mitchell pulled into the lot behind the retirement home and parked the car. Charlie opened the door and got out before he could protest. She took five steps and stumbled. Having enough of her independent demeanor, Mitchell reached out and swept her up into his arms.

"I don't—" she stopped. Her face was inches from his.

He met her gaze head on. "This isn't spending money." He pulled her closer. "It's okay to let people take care of you sometimes."

She studied him as she chewed her lip. The lips that were inches from his. Again, he wondered what they might feel like against his own. Once they were on the porch, he paused. Here, in this moment, it was just the two of them. No Victoria. No ex-boyfriends. Just them.

She took a deep breath and twisted her body. He complied and set her feet on the ground. She took a step toward the door then paused.

"Thank you," she whispered.

He nodded.

Before she turned the handle, the door swung open. Alex stood in the doorway illuminated by the light inside.

"Charlie!" he exclaimed, rushing to her side and taking her arm. "Let's get you inside."

Mitchell watched as she was led to her room. When the door shut, his heart sank.

"Oh, my gosh. You are soaked." Mitchell turned to see Victoria standing there.

"Not now, Vic." He didn't want to go the rounds with her again. He waved her away and headed up the stairs. This trip wasn't going at all how he wanted. Why he'd allowed himself to care for a stranger frustrated him. He was here for Rose and that was it. He couldn't be distracted by the mysterious waitress and caregiver.

He flipped on the water and stepped into the shower. The steaming hot water beat his back, and he welcomed it. It relaxed his tense muscles, and helped him forget about the look on Charlie's face when she'd thought he was Alex.

Shutting off the water, he grabbed a towel. What was their

story anyways? When they'd talked to Francis, Charlie said she didn't have a boyfriend. Well, it didn't look like that anymore.

He wrapped the towel around his waist and pulled open the door. Thankfully, Charlie wasn't standing there to gawk at his chest. Once he was in his room, he paused. Charlie had washed and folded his clothes that he'd dumped in the toilet the day before. Grabbing the shirt, he pulled it on.

Now dressed, he opened the door and made his way downstairs. He could hear voices in the kitchen. As he headed down the hall towards the chatter, he passed by Charlie's room and paused. The door was open, and Alex was standing a bit too close to her.

Jealousy raged through his chest. He wanted to go into the room and punch the guy. He took a step back. Since when did he become a hot head for a girl?

Alex leaned in and brushed his lips against Charlie's, and Mitchell's heart sank. His jaw flexed as he tore his gaze away from them and left the doorway. He leaned against the wall and took a breath. Everything he'd thought about Charlie and him had been all in his head.

She didn't like him. He was such an idiot to think that. He clenched his hands and pushed into the kitchen where Victoria sat at the table. Walking over to her, he pulled her from her seat and grasped each side of her face.

"Mitch—"

He planted a kiss right on her lips. When he pulled away, she looked dazed.

"What was that, Mitchell Kingsley?" she breathed.

"Let's get married." Even when he spoke the words, his stomach churned. If Charlie had feels for Alex, Mitchell needed to get over her right now.

Victoria giggled. "I thought you'd never ask."

The kitchen door swung open and Charlie and Alex walked through. Before either could say anything, Victoria raced over squealing.

"Look what Mitchell just got me." She shoved her hand in front of them and wiggled her fourth finger.

Alex let out a low whistle. "Wowzers. Big rock."

Charlie stared at it for a moment then her gaze drifted over to him. "When—how—?"

"Well, it's been in the works for a while now, but he just asked me. Isn't this the most amazing ring you've ever seen? I'm mean, it's not Tiffany's, but I don't care as long as I'm engaged to my Mitchy," she said as she turned and smiled at him. Clearly she hadn't notice that the questions were aimed at him.

Charlie smiled and headed over to the sink where she filled a glass with water. She stood, facing the window as Mitchell watched her. He couldn't figure out her body language.

Turning, Charlie's smile remained. "I'm happy for you guys. You make a great couple."

Victoria reached out and grasped Mitchell's hand. He glanced at their entwined fingers and nothing in his body felt right. His head raged, and his stomach twisted.

"We are, aren't we," Victoria said as she leaned over. Before he could stop her, she planted another kiss on his lips.

When they pulled away, Charlie was staring at them with a blank expression. "I'm not feeling good. I'm going to lay down."

Mitchell dropped Victoria's hand and stepped toward her. "Are you sure you shouldn't go to the hospital? You could have a concussion."

Charlie raised her hand as if to stop him from coming closer. "I'm fine. I'm just going to go rest in my room."

"I'll come with you," Alex said as he wrapped his arm around her slumped shoulders.

Mitchell watched as she was led from the kitchen. He wanted to stop her, but it didn't matter. She was with Alex, and he was with Victoria.

Turning his attention back to his fiancée, he watched as she pulled out her phone.

"Hello? Mom? It's Victoria. You're never going to believe this!" She sat at the table in full wedding planning mode.

Mitchell didn't want to be here. This was not how he wanted this part of his life to go. His gaze fell to the door that Charlie had just exited.

Feeling confused, he waved at Victoria as he left the room. She was busy chatting, and he doubted she even knew he was gone. He took the stairs to the upper floor two at a time. There was one person he wanted to see.

He stood outside Rose's door and took a breath. Even though she wasn't fully aware, she was still his grandmother and he loved and trusted her. She had always helped him feel better no matter what he'd done.

Turning the handle, he pushed into the room. "Rose?" he called out.

Her bedside light cast a dim glow against the book she was reading. When her gaze met his, she grinned. "Tyler."

He sighed and made his way to the armchair in the corner. He longed for her to recognize him as Mitchell. He missed their relationship as grandson and grandma.

"What's wrong?" she asked, setting her book next to her on the bed.

Collapsing on the chair, he studied her. "Just struggling with life right now."

"Anything specific?" She pulled her glasses off her nose and folded them.

He wanted to tell her about Charlie. About the mistakes he'd made in his life since she'd left. But she looked so earnest that he couldn't bring himself to disappoint her.

"I got engaged." He decided to tell her something he knew would bring her happiness. If she really didn't have much time left, there was no need to focus on the negative.

Just as he thought, her face lit up. "What? To who?"

"Her name is Victoria."

Rose clasped her hands together. "I'm so happy for you. That is just wonderful news."

It felt good to see his grandma smiling, but right now, all he could think about was Charlie. He returned her smile even though inside, his heart was breaking.

CHARLIE

*M*itchell was engaged. That thought made every muscle in Charlie's body ache. Or perhaps, it was because she'd just walloped her head against a huge tree. Either way, she couldn't believe it. It had happened so fast.

Everything she thought they had going on between them had been wrong. Why was she such an idiot sometimes?

"You okay?" Alex's question broke her from her thoughts. He sat next to her on the bed and took her hand in his.

Turning, she peered into his earnest gaze. This was another part of her life that was a complete mess. Why had he kissed her earlier? He was going on and on about how much he missed her then leaned in and she didn't stop him.

"Yeah," she whispered.

Maybe he was sincere. Maybe he had changed. Right now, what other options did she have? She could give him another chance. What did she have to lose?

Leaning in, she met his lips again. His arm wrapped around her. It was true. This was familiar. When she pulled away, she chewed her lip. She just wasn't sure if familiar was what she wanted anymore. She silently cursed herself.

Alex laid back on her bed, staring up at the ceiling. "I've missed you," he said.

She wanted to say the same and had he come a few days earlier, that would have been true. But now, she couldn't find the strength to return his sentiment.

"I should go check on Rose," she said, standing.

"What? Why?" Alex rolled onto his side and propped himself up with his elbow.

"I haven't seen her all day. I just want to make sure she's okay." Truth was, she missed her so much. She wanted to be able to talk to her. Tell her everything that was going wrong in her life. Even if Rose didn't recognize her, just being in her presence would help ease Charlie's confusion.

Alex's phone beeped, and he pulled it out of his pocket. "That's okay. I gotta go anyway."

Charlie nodded as Alex stood. After a quick peck on her cheek he left.

Now alone, Charlie made her way upstairs and down the hall.

Voices could be heard from the open door as she approached Rose's room. She recognized Mitchell's voice and almost turned back. She wasn't sure if she was ready to see him again. But then she shook it off. He was Rose's family which meant he was going to be around a lot. Which meant being here with his new wife. Charlie needed to get over her crush and move on.

She knocked on the door and slipped through the opening. Her eyes widened as she took in the sight. Rose was out of bed and standing next to a huge pile of clothes. Her eyes lit up when she looked at Charlie.

"Is this her?" she asked, turning to Mitchell.

His gaze snapped over to Charlie. He paused then shook his head. "No."

"Oh," Rose said as she turned back to the clothes.

Trying to ignore the pain in her heart, Charlie approached her. "It's so good to see you're out of bed."

Rose turned, and she had a no nonsense look on her face. "Of course. I need to pick out what I'm going to wear to my son's wedding."

Charlie's gaze flew over to Mitchell. He'd told her already? Maybe they were really that serious. His smile dropped a bit as he studied her.

It was too overwhelming for her to try and analyze his gaze. Instead, she turned her attention back to Rose. "That's a good reason."

Rose laughed. It had been ages since Charlie had heard it. Tears brimmed on her lids. It was a wonderful sound.

"When's the wedding?" she asked.

Mitchell shrugged. "I'm not sure. We haven't picked a date."

Rose stopped. "I'm coming, right?"

"Of course," he said.

Charlie turned back to him. Why was he making promises that he knew he couldn't keep? Most weddings took at least a year to plan. With Victoria's personality, it would probably be twice that. Rose would most likely be gone by then. Even if she wouldn't remember the promise, there was a chance she might. He couldn't disappoint her like that.

"Don't make promises you can't keep," Charlie whispered to him.

Mitchell raised an eyebrow as he studied her. "What are you talking about?"

"You're promising she'll be there. I've never seen her this excited. If you leave without fulfilling that promise, I'm worried what that'll do to her." Charlie grinned back at Rose who was holding a dark red dress up to herself.

When Charlie turned her gaze back to Mitchell, her cheeks heated from the intense look in his eyes. "What do you suggest I do?" he whispered.

She wanted to tell him to break off the engagement, but that was ridiculous. He loved Victoria—not her. "Have it here," slipped out.

His eyebrows shot up.

"You're getting married here?" Rose asked with so much hope and excitement in her voice.

"What? I..." Mitchell glanced from Charlie back to Rose.

Rose set the dress down and walked over to him. Grabbing his hand in hers, she smiled at him. "There's nothing in this world I want more than to see my son get married here."

Mitchell's jaw flexed as he studied Rose. Charlie felt completely stupid for blurting that out, but if they were going to get married and wanted Rose there, it had to be here and it had to be soon. If seeing her son get married brought her happiness, Charlie would make sure it happened.

"Okay," Mitchell said. "We'll have it here."

Rose smiled and went back to sorting her clothes.

"Um, Charlie, can I see you in the hall?" He stood and nodded toward the door.

"Sure." She didn't want to, but it was inevitable. They might as well get it all out in the open.

Once she was out in the hall, she closed the door behind her and turned.

Mitchell was staring down at her. A mixture of frustration and confusion in his gaze. "What was that?"

Charlie leaned against the wall and folded her arms. It would be better to keep as much distance between them as possible. "What was what?"

"That. In there." He waved to the door and began pacing.

"You made the promise. I was just making sure you stuck to your word."

He stopped, inches from her. "Is that what you want?"

No. But she couldn't say that. Not when Rose seemed to be returning to her naturally cheery self. "Listen. You love Victoria, right?"

Mitchell studied her for a moment then nodded.

Her heart sank, but she continued. "And you love Rose, right?"

He nodded again, this time more vigorously.

"Then why does it matter where you get married or when? I'd say do it here and do it as soon as possible."

His gaze drifted from her face over to the window. "Is that what you think is best?" There was a deepness to his voice that she couldn't quite figure out.

She rubbed her arms. "It's what I think is best for everyone."

His focus remained on something outside. "Alright. I'll go let Victoria know." He turned and made his way down the hall.

Once he was gone, she let out the breath she'd been holding. Every part of her wanted to run after him and tell him she didn't want him to marry Victoria. But she couldn't crush Rose's happiness like that.

Her stomach clenched as she chewed her nail. Did she think that he'd marry her instead? If there was a chance that seeing her grandson get married would bring Rose back, even for a moment, Charlie would do whatever was necessary to make it happen.

She pushed off the wall and made her way downstairs. A resolve grew in her chest as she slipped into her room. She didn't want to do it, but she couldn't ignore the nagging in her mind. For everyone around her to be happy, it was time she started forgetting the billionaire.

Charlie woke the next morning to a loud knock on the front door. Waving her hand to make it go away, she turned and pulled a pillow over her head. It was Saturday. The day Penny took over the chores so she could sleep in, and she wasn't ready to get up just yet.

The knock came again—more forceful this time.

Penny must be busy in the kitchen. "Alright, I'm up," she yelled as she rolled off the bed. Grabbing her robe, she left her room.

The knock continued as she approached. She opened the door, stopping the man mid-knock.

"What are you doing here at"— she glanced over at the clock on the wall— "nine in the morning?" Was it really that late?

"I'm sorry to bother you, miss—"

"Charlie."

"Charlie, but I have a delivery for you."

She glanced behind him to the huge, white delivery truck in the driveway. "Delivery. What are you talking about? I haven't ordered anything."

The man had on a blue uniform and held a clipboard which he was riffling through. "It says here you ordered ten twin mattresses."

Charlie's stomach sank. She did what? "I'm sorry. There must have been a mistake. I didn't order anything." She couldn't afford new mattresses right now.

The man glanced at her then back to his truck. "I'm not sure. I'm just the driver. They load up my truck, and I deliver them."

"Take them back. I didn't order them, and I certainly can't pay for them."

His shook his head. "I can't. I have to deliver. If you have a problem, you're going to have to call corporate."

He waved his hand toward two other men who were milling around the back of the truck. At his signal, they pulled open the back and began pulling mattress out.

The sound of paper ripping brought Charlie's focus back to the man. He handed her the slip and bounded down the steps.

This was the last thing she needed. What was she going to do with ten mattresses while she figured out who made this mistake?

"Sir, you can't do this." Charlie raced down the steps.

The man was directing the others to the front door.

"Hey!" She reached out and grabbed his arm. "I'm talking to you."

He glanced down at her. "I know. I'm sorry, but this is my job. I can't go back with these in my truck."

She threw up her hands. "Well, what am I supposed to do with ten mattresses?"

He shrugged. "Use them?"

"Use them!" She sputtered as she clenched her fists.

"What's going on?" Mitchell asked as he crossed the grass and approached her.

Charlie groaned. This was not what she needed. "It's nothing."

His gaze ran over her, and his annoyingly charming half-smile emerged. "Doesn't look like nothing."

"This man thinks I ordered ten mattresses and isn't listening to me. I didn't order them." She turned and shouted to the men who seemed to have picked up speed. No doubt they wanted to finish and leave.

"Oh."

Charlie whipped around. "What do you mean, oh?"

Mitchell gave her a sheepish smile. "I actually ordered them."

Her cheeks heated as she stared at him. "What?"

"It was before you made me promise not to spend my money on you. I ordered new mattresses for all the residents."

Charlie clenched her fists. It was sweet and infuriating at the same time. "Why would you do that?"

He shrugged.

The last mattress passed by in front of them. The man from earlier approached her. "We'll pick up the old mattress if you decide you want to keep these. Just call the store." Then all three men sprinted across the lawn and the truck roared to life. When they were gone, Charlie turned.

"Please, just keep them." Mitchell shoved his hands into the front pockets of his jeans and gave her an earnest look.

She chewed the inside of her cheek. It did seem easier then

calling up corporate to have them come pick the mattresses up. She sighed and made her way across the yard. "Fine. With one condition, you let me pay you back."

"What? No, it—"

She raised her hand. "I insist."

He paused then nodded. "Okay."

Smiling, she made her way into the house and back to the kitchen where Penny had left a few pancakes and sausages on a plate for her. She threw it into the microwave just as Mitchell walked in.

"What do you guys have planned for today?" She grabbed out a fork and the microwave dinged. He sat down on a chair next to the table. Not wanting to be too close to him, she grabbed her plate out and leaned against the counter.

"Vic left for New York last night."

Charlie coughed as a crumb flew to the back of her throat. "What? She got a flight fast."

"She has a plane."

Charlie nodded as she filled up a glass and took a swig. Of course, these were people with money. "When will she be back?" Secretly, she hoped he'd tell her that they were over.

"Monday. She had some things to get done for the wedding. A dress. That sort of thing."

Charlie chewed as she nodded, thankful for the distraction eating gave her. "Monday, huh. That's fast."

"Well, the wedding is on Tuesday."

This time, a whole chunk of pancake flew to the back of her throat and a coughing fit ensued.

Mitchell stood. "You okay?"

She held up her hand and nodded as tears streamed down her face. Once the coughs settled, she took another drink. "Tuesday, huh?" she rasped.

He nodded. "Well, you told us to do it here and fast. She wasn't too happy about it, but I gave her a budget that helped convince her."

After sopping up the last bit of syrup with her pancake, she placed her plate in the sink. If he was willing to give Jorge a quarter of a million, she could only image what his wedding budget looked like.

"Oh good, you're still here," a familiar voice said.

Charlie spun around, not believing what she heard. Her heart raced as she blinked, hoping that what she saw was true. Rose was standing in the doorway. She was dressed and had a huge smile on her face.

"Rose?" Charlie approached her.

Rose looked at her, and her eyebrows furrowed. "Yes. Do I know you?"

Charlie inched closer. "It's me, Charlie. You're out of bed."

Rose laughed. "Of course, I am. I wouldn't miss planning my son's wedding."

"You remembered?" Charlie stopped.

If Rose remembered, then that meant things might be getting better. If that were true then no matter how much this wedding broke Charlie's heart, it needed to continue.

MITCHELL

*M*itchell watched Charlie stare at Rose with a dazed look on her face.

"Yes, I remembered. How could I forget my only son's big news?" She crossed the kitchen and held out her hand for Mitchell to take. "I can't wait to start planning."

Mitchell took her hand and smiled at her. It felt good to see his grandmother excited about something.

Just as he was about to reply, his phone rang. He pulled it from his pocket and glanced down. It was his mom. He'd been trying to get a hold of her all night.

"I need to take this," he said as he stood. He waved at his seat for Rose to take. She smiled and sat. Charlie remained on the other side of the room, staring at her.

"Mom?" Mitchell asked as he stepped into the hall.

"Mitchell? What's wrong? Why have you been calling me non-stop."

He leaned against the wall. "I wanted you to be one of the first to know."

She sighed. "Know what, Mitchell? I'm about to step into a meeting."

Just like his mom—always working.

"Well, I just figured my mom would want to know when her son gets engaged."

Silence.

"To whom?" she asked.

He pushed off the wall and began tracing the wallpaper flowers with his finger. "Victoria."

"Oh, good."

That was it? "And we're getting married on Tuesday."

He heard sputtering on the other end.

"Tuesday? Oh, no Mitchell. Is she pregnant?"

"What? Mom, no."

"Then why so soon?"

He swallowed and steadied his nerves. She was not going to like what he was about to say. "I want Rose there. That's why we're having it here. In Sitka."

Even though there was silence on the other end, he could feel the rage that flowed through her. "No, Mitchell. Absolutely not."

He gritted his teeth. "It's not up to you, Mother."

"I forbid it."

"You can't—" He took a deep breath. "You can't forbid it. It's happening here whether you like it or not."

Silence.

"I hope you can put the past behind you and come. It would mean a lot to me."

"I have to go." Her voice was cool and distant.

"Okay. I love you, Mother."

"Goodbye, Mitchell."

He went to say goodbye, but stopped when he heard a click. Staring at the phone, Mitchell fought the urge to call her back and give her a piece of his mind. What kind of mom did that? He smirked as he shoved his phone into his pocket. Oh, that's right, his mom.

Taking a deep breath, he entered the kitchen where Charlie

and Rose were now sitting next to each other and they were laughing.

Charlie's gaze fell to him, and her expression grew soft. "You okay?"

He forced a smile and nodded. "Yeah. Just business."

Rose turned and gave him another loving smile. "You were always such a hard worker."

He pulled the chair out and sat across from them. "What were you ladies talking about?"

Charlie smiled as she leaned forward. "Rose is telling me about all the shops she wants to take you to for the wedding." She leaned closer. "She's actually remembering," she whispered.

He couldn't help but smile at the giddiness that seeped from her gaze. "Oh, really. Like what shops?"

"Samson's for the cake. Oh, and we can get Jorge to cater the dinner," Rose began ticking names off on her fingers.

Mitchell glanced over at Charlie whose lips were opened in an "o". She turned and mouthed "Oh, my gosh". The edges of her eyes crinkled as she grinned.

"Well, we should go then." He stood and held out his hand for Rose.

"What? Now?" she asked as she took it and he helped her stand.

"Of course, there's no time like the present." He bent his elbow, and she slipped her hand in.

"Okay, then," she said.

With Charlie following behind them, he led her out of the house and over to his car. Rose squinted against the sunlight.

"The sun's out. That's a good sign. God's smiling today," she said as he opened the door, and helped her onto the passenger seat.

He rounded the car. He wanted to catch Charlie before she got in.

She had her hand on the handle, but hadn't yet pulled it open.

"Hey," he said, reaching out and stilling her hand. Electricity shot up his arm from how soft her skin felt on his fingers. He pulled away as if he'd been burned.

She dropped her hand off the handle and turned. The look on her face told him she had felt it too. But he couldn't delve into those thoughts again, so he just gave her a smile.

"This is good, right?" He nodded toward Rose.

Charlie chewed her lip and nodded. He could see the tears that brimmed on her lids. "It's good. I haven't seen her remember this much in a long time."

He wanted to wrap Charlie up in his arms and hold her. But he fought that desire. "It's awesome."

Charlie smiled. "Yes."

She moved to grab the handle, but he reached out. "Let me." He opened the door and waved her inside.

"I can open my own door." She shot him a disapproving look.

He leaned in until he was inches from her ear. "I know."

She stiffened and slid into the car. He smiled. He enjoyed that he could make her squirm. He shut the door then got behind the wheel.

"Alrighty, ladies. Where to?"

Shopping with Rose and Charlie was so much better than with Victoria. They'd stopped by Jorge's and asked him to cater the wedding which he was more than happy to do. He kicked all the customers out of the restaurant and had the kitchen whip together an assortment of appetizers and entrees.

Once they had tried everything, Jorge wrote up the order then all three of them left, complaining about how full their stomachs were.

Now they sat in front of a balding, portly man. Samson was apparently the best baker in town.

"No, no. I cannot. It's too soon." Samson tapped his fingers on his desk as he shook his head.

"Come on, it's for Rose." Charlie waved her hand toward Rose.

Samson studied them then shrugged. "But it's too soon. I only have three days to concoct my famous creations. No. It's too soon."

Mitchell shifted to remove his wallet. "How about I sweeten the pot a bit." He pulled open a fold and fiddled with the bills.

Charlie cleared her throat and shot him a look. "Please, Samson. Do it for us. Do it for Rose."

Samson stared at her then sighed. "Fine. For Rose. I still haven't found a better cake decorator since she retired."

Charlie leaned back and grinned "Perfect."

"Maria! Samples," Samson said as he turned and pushed open the swinging door behind him.

"Yes," a female voice responded.

Rose stood and wandered around the shop, glancing at all the baked goods that were lined up in the glass enclosures.

Charlie leaned over to him. "What was that?"

Mitchell shrugged and shoved his wallet back into his pocket. "What?"

"Remember what I said about using your money to solve problems? Do you ever just talk to people?"

He rubbed his hand on his pant leg. It was strange to be around a woman who wanted nothing to do with his money. Everyone he'd ever dated stayed with him because of it.

"I talk to people," he said. "Money just helps."

Charlie leaned over. "Life isn't always about money." Then she stood and made her way over to Rose. They started talking and pointing at cupcakes.

What did she know? His whole life had revolved around the numbers in his bank account. To his mom and dad, it was the thing they cherished the most. To him, it was the only thing that seemed to bring him happiness. Why would he stop now?

A thin woman with a white apron pushed through the door with a tray of cake slices balanced on her shoulder. Rose and Charlie made their way back to Samson's desk and sat. After they'd sampled all the varieties, Mitchell settled on vanilla with raspberry filling.

Samson took his order and promised he'd have it ready. As they left the bakery and began walking down the sidewalk, Mitchell noticed that Rose looked confused.

"You okay?" he asked.

She glanced back at the cake shop. "That place. It felt familiar."

Charlie fell in step with her. "Really? How?" There was a hint of hope in her voice.

Rose studied Charlie. Her brows furrowed as she turned back to the bakery. "I'm not sure." Her face fell. "I'm tired. Take me home?"

Mitchell glanced over at Charlie. All the hope that was there was gone.

"Are you sure, Rose?" she asked.

Rose slipped her arm through Mitchell's and nodded. "Yes."

They walked over to his car and got in. No one spoke as they drove back to the retirement home.

Once Rose was in her room and tucked into bed, Charlie shut the door. Mitchell studied her. She looked forlorn. He wanted to reach out and pull her into a hug, but as a newly engaged man, that wouldn't look good. Instead, he shoved his hands into his pockets and leaned against the wall.

"What's going on?" he asked. Questions never hurt anyone.

Charlie looked up. "What do you mean?"

"You look sad."

Sighing, she glanced at her watch. "I was hoping when she recognized the bakery that it would lead to something. But I guess not. When she wakes up we'll be right back to where we've always been." Her gaze flicked over to him before it rested on the window at the end of the hall. "It just gets draining, you know?"

He nodded. "Yeah. I don't know how you do it. Most people would have given up."

She chewed her lip. He smiled. He was beginning to love the little quirks she did when she was nervous.

"What?" She furrowed her brow when she glanced over at him.

"What?" he asked.

"You're grinning at me," she said.

Mitchell couldn't help it. She was adorable. "You chew your lip when you're nervous or worried."

She straightened her face. "No I don't."

He shrugged. "Okay."

"I don't."

Mitchell raised his hands. "Okay. You don't."

She glared at him, but it slowly turned into a smile. "What are your plans for the rest of the evening?"

Pulling out his phone, he glanced at the time. "One o'clock. Hmm, don't have a lot going on."

"I was thinking about going to the music festival today. Want to join me?"

Perhaps it was just his desire for her to want to spend time with him, but he swore she blushed.

He rubbed his chin. He couldn't accept right away. She'd sense how desperate he was. "What does one do at this festival?"

"Normal carnival things. Games, loads of food. Oh, and listening to bands play."

"I don't know..."

Her face fell as she studied him. "It's okay, I unders—"

Mitchell laughed. "No. It's not that. I just don't know if you can handle getting whooped by me. I'm a champion when it comes to carnival games."

Her eyebrows shot up. "Oh, really."

Mitchell pushed off the wall and flexed his arms. "Do you think I have these babies for no reason?" He leaned over and kissed a bicep.

She giggled and rolled her eyes. "We'll just see about that." She started making her way down the hall. "I'm gonna go change. I'll meet you in the kitchen in fifteen?"

"It's a date," he said. Just to watch her squirm.

She paused and glanced over at him.

"Joking." But deep down, he wasn't.

She smiled and disappeared down the stairs.

As he walked into his room, his phone rang. Pulling it out of his pocket he hit talk. "Hello?"

"Mr. Kingsley?"

"Yep?"

"This is Thomas McMillan with Royal Yacht rentals."

"Oh, yeah. Hi."

"I'm returning your phone call. You were inquiring about one of our boats for an upcoming wedding?"

Mitchell sat down on his bed. One of Victoria's stipulations for getting married in Alaska was that they at least had the reception on a yacht. He'd called this morning hoping there was something available. "Yes. We're getting married on Tuesday."

Thomas sputtered then coughed to cover it up. "Wow. That's soon."

"Yeah. Listen, money isn't a problem. I'll pay what's needed to get this done."

"Sounds good. We actually have a yacht docking this evening. Do you have some time to come aboard and take a look?"

Mitchell gritted his teeth. Truth was, he really didn't. He wanted to spend the whole day with Charlie. "Can I get back to you?"

"Sure. You can call me or just head down to Old Sitka dock when you get a chance. The boat is called King of the Court. I'll let them know you might be coming."

"Thanks." He hung up and shoved his phone back into his pocket. Slipping off his shirt, he dug through his clean clothes. His thoughts returned to Charlie. One thing was for sure, he wanted to look good tonight.

CHARLIE

*C*harlie stood in front of her closet, staring at her clothes. Nothing seemed good enough for the festival. Sighing, she grabbed her yellow sundress from its hanger. She was acting ridiculous. This was Mitchell— the guy she couldn't have.

Pulling off her jeans and t-shirt, she slipped the dress on. It helped highlight the little bit of color she'd managed to get during the small bursts of sunlight. She released her hair from its bun. The curls fell to the middle of her back.

The gash on her forehead was starting to bruise so she focused her efforts on covering it up. After a few brushes of foundation and mascara she was ready. Just as she stepped out of her room, her phone rang.

It was Alex.

"Hello?"

"Charlie?"

"Yep."

"Hey. I stopped by earlier, and you weren't home. Penny said you were out wedding shopping?"

Charlie leaned against the door frame. "Yeah. I'm helping Rose's grandson plan his wedding."

"The guy from yesterday?"

"Yep."

"Huh."

Charlie wasn't sure, but she thought that she detected a hint of jealousy in Alex's tone. "He's getting married on Tuesday, so I was showing him around."

"Oh. Are you free now?"

She chewed her bottom lip. "We were about to head out to the music festival."

"We meaning, you and this guy?"

"It's not like that," she said. "You're free to come."

"Well, I don't want to get in the way."

Why was he acting like this? "You won't be in the way. Please, it'll be fun."

"Okay."

"See you there?"

"Sure."

Charlie hung up. She couldn't ignore how the conversation had left a sour feeling in her stomach. What did he have to be jealous about? Mitchell was spoken for. It wasn't like anything could happen. Right?

She pushed the kitchen door open and inwardly groaned. Why did Mitchell have to look so good all of the time? He had on a navy button-up shirt and light jeans. His hair was gelled. She sighed. Maybe Alex did have a reason to be jealous.

His gaze ran over her and there was a look of approval in his eyes. Heat raced to her cheeks. She should have just worn a potato sack. Now what would Alex think? That she was trying to impress Mitchell?

"Ready?" she asked as she made her way past him to the back-door. As she neared, she caught a whiff of his cologne. It made her insides turn to mush. This was too much. Maybe she could feign sickness and stay in bed.

He followed after her, blocking the retreat to her room. "Yep. Ready to get whooped by me?"

Must not flirt. Must not flirt, she chanted in her mind.

"Alex is coming," she blurted out. Maybe that would help them keep their distance from each other.

Mitchell was silent. "Really? Why?"

She grabbed her sandals from the entryway and bent down to slip them on. She teetered on one foot while she shoved the other one into a shoe. A warm hand rested on her lower back.

"Whoa," he said, his voice lower than normal.

Startled, she glanced over to see Mitchell staring down at her. His look and the sensation of his hand on her back was too much, so she straightened. "I'm okay." She shot her hand out and rested it on the wall to help her balance.

"I'm sorry. Just didn't want you to fall over." He shoved his hands into his front pockets.

"No. It's okay." Why did her voice have to sound so squeaky?

He peered over at her then nodded. "So Alex is coming?"

She pulled open the door and stepped out. The sun was shining against the dark clouds that loomed in the east. "My boyfriend, Alex, is coming." She wasn't sure if she was reminding Mitchell or herself.

He followed behind her. "Got it."

They walked across the parking lot to Mitchell's car. They still hadn't gone back for hers. The memory of him coming to her rescue yesterday flooded her mind.

"Thanks," she said.

His gaze met hers. "For what?"

"Coming to find me yesterday."

He pulled open her door and smiled. "Of course. We're friends. We look out for each other."

She slipped onto the seat. "Yes…friends," she said as she pulled the door shut.

Mitchell jogged around the front of the car and got in. "I'll take you to get your car if you want."

"It's okay. We can get it tonight."

He peered over to her as he turned the key. "You sure?"

She nodded. As much as she wanted to have a vehicle close in case she needed a quick getaway, she kind of liked the idea that she *had* to ride back home with him. She enjoyed his company.

As he pulled onto the main road, he rested his wrist on the wheel. "So, what's the story about you and Alex? Last time I'd heard, you were single."

She brushed down her skirt and stared outside. "He was my boyfriend for three years."

"Three? Wow. What happened?"

Her stomach twisted at the memory. "I caught him making out with another girl."

For a split second, she thought she saw his knuckles whiten as he gripped the steering wheel.

"And you want him back?" he asked.

Charlie sighed. She wasn't sure at all. All she knew was, this was a small town. If she didn't take him, who else would want her? Certainly not the handsome visitor sitting next to her.

"He's changed. I've changed. I want to believe we can make it work."

He flicked on his blinker and pulled into the grassy field that had been turned into a parking lot. After shutting off his car, he faced her. "Do you love him?"

She almost choked from his direct question. "Yes," she squeaked out.

Mitchell's brows furrowed as he stared at her. "I'm happy for you," he said as pulled on his door handle.

Charlie did the same. She rounded the front of the car as he hit the button and the doors locked. "Thank you. I'm happy for you, too." She smiled.

They walked in silence. The music that blared from the speakers next to the stage helped lessen the awkwardness she felt.

Her phone dinged. She pulled it out of her purse and glanced down at it.

"Alex is by the ring toss." She nodded in the direction of the game booths.

"Okay," Mitchell said, following after her.

She walked until she saw Alex waving.

"Hey," she said, as she approached him.

He grinned, wrapped his arm around her waist, and kissed her cheek.

Charlie let her gaze fall to Mitchell. His jaw flexed as he stared a bit too hard at the game behind them.

"Mitchell, glad you could join us," Alex said, pulling her even closer.

Mitchell turned his attention to Alex. He had a frustrated look. "Well, she invited me before you so, thanks for joining us."

Alex let out a laugh. "Okay."

Charlie needed to change the subject. "Are you gonna play?" She nodded to the set of rings around Alex's free hand.

"Yep. I was about to win you that stuffed bear." He motioned to the oversized polar bear that hung from the booth.

"Really?" Charlie tried to hide her excitement. Polar bears were her favorite animal. "You remembered."

Alex leaned over and gave her another kiss on the cheek. "Of course, I remembered. They're your favorite."

He unwrapped his arm and began tossing the rings toward the bottles. Five clinked as they bounced off the glass and fell to the ground. He only managed to get three on.

"Oh, no. Better luck next time," the pimply teenager who ran the booth said.

"It's okay." Charlie smiled over at Alex.

He looked frustrated, but shrugged. "Let's try another game."

"Hang on. Let me try," Mitchell said, stepping up to the attendant and pulling out his wallet.

Charlie forced a giggle. "It's okay. I really don't need it." What was he doing?

"If they're your favorite animal, let me try." He grabbed the rings that the attendant had dropped on the counter.

"Really, it's okay." Charlie stepped forward. Alex was a really competitive guy. Things wouldn't go over well if he lost.

But Mitchell ignored her and began throwing the rings. As the fifth one sailed through the air and spun as it landed on the bottle, Charlie's stomach plummeted. She could feel Alex tense. Once all eight were tossed, the attendant counted them up and declared Mitchell a winner.

"Which toy do you want?" he asked through his bubblegum.

Mitchell grinned at Charlie. She glared at him.

"The polar bear," he said, nodding toward the white animal.

The attendant pulled it down and handed it to him then headed off to help a family.

"Here," Mitchell said, holding out the bear.

"I'm gonna get a drink," Alex said. His voice was flat.

Once he was gone, Charlie whipped around. "What was that?" Heat raced up her spine as she did her best to stare him down.

Mitchell just shrugged which angered her more. "What was what?" he asked.

"Why did you have to do that? Show Alex up."

Mitchell sighed. "Will you just take the bear?"

Charlie folded her arms. "No."

He leaned in. "I won it for you."

"Yeah. Well, I didn't ask you to."

Mitchell scrubbed his stubble with his free hand. "I know you didn't, but it wasn't like Alex was going to be able to win it."

"So? He's my boyfriend." She turned. With the way she was feeling, she needed some ice cream.

"Why? If he cheated on you, why would you take him back?" Mitchell asked, following after her.

Now he was giving her relationship advice? "Who are you to ask? It's not like there are a ton of guys on this island. All of them are either taken or recently engaged." She dropped her gaze. She hadn't meant for that to slip out.

When he didn't respond, she glanced up. He was studying her. She wished she could read his thoughts.

"Don't get me wrong, I'm happy for you." She swallowed, hoping she sounded sincere. "And it has been amazing seeing Rose come back. There's nothing I want more than to see you get married. It's bringing her so much happiness."

Mitchell rubbed his neck as he glanced around. "Yeah, it is."

Charlie gave him a smile. She didn't want to fight. "If helping you with this wedding is going to bring her back, then I wouldn't have it any other way." She nodded toward the stuffed animal. "Give it to Victoria. I'm sure she'll love it."

He glanced down at the bear as if he'd forgotten it was in his hand. He paused then smiled up at her. "I'm sorry for being such a jerk. I can be a hot head sometimes. It's just that…" His gaze deepened. "I care about you. I don't want to see you get hurt."

Charlie's stomach leapt to her throat at his words. She swallowed, forcing herself to calm down. He probably only cared about her like he would a little sister. "I care about you, too. I'm happy you've found Victoria. She suits you."

Her gaze fell behind him to Alex who was approaching with two drinks in hand. She smiled at him. It seemed to help him lighten up a bit. When he joined them, he handed her a glass.

"I got one for you," he said, leaning over and giving her a kiss.

"Hey, man, I want to say I'm sorry. I can get a little competitive sometimes. I'm going to keep this bear for my fiancée, so if Charlie wants one, you're going to have to win it for her." He shoved the bear under his arm.

Alex nodded, but then a familiar look flitted across his face. "If you like competition so much, my buddies and I like to compete in the lumberjack competition. We're practicing tomorrow. What do you think?" He leaned forward.

"Alex." Charlie shook her head. "Mitchell doesn't want to do that."

Mitchell's eyebrows shot up. "What's a lumberjack competition?"

"It's where we use axes and chainsaws to compete. Just like loggers used to do."

Charlie needed to intervene. "It's silly. Don't feel like you have to do it. These guys practice all the time. It can get dangerous." Why was Alex doing this?

Mitchell stared at her then back to Alex. "I'll do it. I'm a quick learner."

Alex broke out into a grin. "Awesome. We'll come get you tomorrow." He turned to Charlie. "Let's do the bean bag toss. I'll win you a bear there. I'm better at that anyway." He started for the booth.

Charlie followed after him, and Mitchell fell into step with her. "You don't have to do this you know," she said, turning to look at him.

His jaw flexed as he focused on the ground ahead. "I know," he said as he stepped up to the booth and bought a bucket of beanbags.

Charlie folded her arms. This was not what she wanted. The lumberjack competition could get dangerous, and she didn't know what she'd do if something happened to Mitche—Alex. She meant Alex.

14

MITCHELL

*M*itchell didn't like Alex. What did Charlie see in him anyway? There was nothing redeeming about him. And it wasn't just because he'd had his arm wrapped around Charlie's waist for the last hour. Or the fact that'd he was on his fifth drink, and his speech was starting to slur. It took all of Mitchell's strength not to deck the guy.

The three of them played every carnival game at the festival. It wasn't until the last one that Alex finally won Charlie a stuffed animal. It wasn't a bear as they'd run out of those already.

Mitchell tried not to huff as Alex handed her a gorilla. She gave him a shy smile and kissed his cheek. Mitchell stared at the bear he'd won her. Great. Now he was stuck with this constant reminder that he couldn't have the intoxicating girl who was giggling next to him.

Where was Victoria? He actually missed having her around. At least then he wouldn't be the third wheel.

"Hot dogs?" He nodded toward the booth in front of them.

Charlie turned to him. "Sure."

They walked up to the stand. Mitchell ordered a foot long and almost told them to hold the onions but then paused. Why did he care if he smelled? Charlie wasn't getting close to him tonight, so he ordered a double helping.

Alex stepped up and ordered for Charlie. Mitchell glared at him. She had a problem when he bought stuff for her but not Alex? The thought made him clench his fist. What was with him? His temperature had skyrocketed. He needed to cool down. He opened his Sprite and downed half.

"That's ten dollars," the booth attendant said as he handed them the hot dogs they had ordered.

Alex pulled out his wallet. He fumbled for a minute before turning to Charlie. "Hey babe, can you spot me on this? I think I spent my last few dollars winning that for you." He nodded to the gorilla.

Mitchell watched Charlie's face fall. "Um, yeah. I think so." She handed the stuffed animal to him and rifled around in her purse. When she looked up, Mitchell's heart hurt for her. She looked so disappointed.

"I've got it," he said, stepping up to the counter and pulling a twenty out of his wallet. "Give us a few sodas while you're at it."

"Mitchell, no—" Charlie started.

He narrowed his eyes at her. This was getting ridiculous. He had no idea what he'd done to deserve her reservations. "It's okay. I've got it," he repeated

Alex smiled, snaked his filthy arm around her waist, and pulled her close again. "It's okay, babe. He's got it."

Mitchell forced a smile, but then glared at Alex. Man, he hated that guy.

With the food paid for, they headed over to the booths decked out in all different band garb. There were posters and cd's for sale.

"Alex, we should go. We don't have any more money." Charlie grabbed his arm to stop him.

Mitchell raised his hand. He didn't want the evening to end. Even if spending time with Charlie meant spending time with Alex— he'd do it. "It's okay. I'll cover us."

Charlie chewed her lip. "I couldn't ask you to do that."

Mitchell reached into his wallet and pulled out a few hundred dollar bills. "Hey, you know the day I came into the diner and got you fired? Well, I forgot to tip you. Here." He reached out and shoved the money into her hand.

She stared at the bills then back to him. "This is way too much."

Alex let out a low whistle. "Geez, that's a big tip." He pulled Charlie closer and leaned in. "Just take it, baby," he said with his voice low.

Charlie stared at Alex then back to Mitchell. He couldn't quite read the look on her face. Suddenly, she clenched her jaw and threw the bills at him.

"I told you, this is too much." Then she turned and practically ran away.

Mitchell watched her. It was obvious that he'd upset her, but why boggled his mind.

"What's with her?" Alex asked, turning to look at him.

Mitchell shrugged.

Alex moved toward the bills. "I'll, um, give these to her."

Mitchell glared at Alex, but didn't stop him. Instead, he headed after Charlie. A phone rang out. He patted his pocket, but it wasn't his. Turning, he noticed Alex coming up from behind.

"Hello?" Alex raised his phone to his cheek.

Mitchell tried to ignore him and kept his gaze focused on Charlie's retreating frame.

"Right now?" Alex paused then nodded. "I'll be there." He shoved his phone into his pocket. "Hey, man. I got a fishing job for the night. Can you tell Charlie for me? Tell her I'll see her tomorrow."

Mitchell nodded. Good. He was ready for this loser to be gone.

Alex veered off toward the parking lot leaving Mitchell alone. It didn't take long before he found Charlie sitting on a rock. She was staring off toward the ocean with her arms wrapped around her chest. He approached slowly, not sure how she'd react when she saw that he had followed her.

"I see you," she sighed.

He straightened and headed over to her. "You okay?"

She scoffed. "Where's Alex?" she asked as she rubbed her skin as if she were cold. He fought the urge to wrap his arms around her to warm her up just as he had done when he found her in the woods.

"He had to leave. Got a fishing job."

Her gaze focused on him. "A what?"

Mitchell settled on a smaller rock next to her. "A fishing job?" he repeated himself.

"Huh." She turned her gaze outward again. "Why do you keep doing that?"

"Doing what?" he asked even though he was pretty sure he knew what she meant.

"Shoving your money at me. Showing Alex up. He's a competitive guy."

"You were hungry and, like I said, you should let people help you sometimes." He wasn't going to apologize for having money. He worked hard for it. He basically kept his family's business running.

Her face stilled. "What's life like for you?"

He stared at her. "What do you mean?"

"Tell me what a day is like for you. Paint the picture of what a billionaire does." She shook her head as if the word "billionaire" tasted weird on her tongue.

He focused on the water. "I work. A lot. Real estate doesn't just buy and sell itself. I'm in meetings all the time. Sometimes until the wee hours of the morning."

"Sounds sad." Her gaze softened.

He shrugged. "You get used to it."

"What about relationships? You know, besides Victoria?"

He nudged a rock with his toe. He enjoyed having her ask him personal questions like this. It made their relationship real. He wanted her to know everything about him even if the answers were hard to say. "It's hard. When people hear I have money suddenly they don't see me as a person anymore. I'm a dollar amount. It's like they are trying to get the most out of me. I always doubt the real reason they're my friend."

She glanced over at him. He saw sympathy in her gaze. "It's hard to know who's genuine," she breathed out as if she understood.

His heart surged at her words. Victoria never asked these kinds of questions. Money was all the mattered to her. Anger filled his chest. Why was he with her again?

"I won't do that," Charlie said, not breaking his gaze.

He furrowed his brow. "Do what?"

"Take advantage of you. I promise I will always see you as a person and not your money." She reached out and brushed his hand with her fingertips.

He swallowed. Tingles raced up his arm at her touch. He opened his mouth to speak. There was a question he needed to ask her. If he broke it off with Victoria, did they have a chance? The words settled on the tip of his tongue. Now would be the perfect time.

"And I'll be here when you come back to see Rose, you know, after you and Victoria are married." She dropped her hand and smiled at him. "Rose is excited about your wedding. Her happiness is important to me." Her gaze intensified as if she suspected what he was going to say, but didn't want him to voice it.

His heart tightened like a vice in his chest. "Victoria, yeah. It'll be nice."

She stuck out her hand. "Friends?"

He eyed it. "Only if you promise to always be honest with me." Then he paused. "And you let me pay for the rest of the night."

She hesitated.

"Please?"

"Okay." A smile played on her lips.

He grabbed her hand and tried to ignore the fireworks that shot through him every time he touched her. "Deal."

He stood, still clutching her hand in his, and helped her to her feet.

"Come on. They're bobbing for apples. It's been my favorite game since I was a kid," he said.

Her giggle raced through him. He debated about keeping ahold of her hand, but then dropped it. She'd already set the parameters of their relationship, and he was pretty sure holding hands wasn't something "just friends" did.

They walked in silence as they headed toward the booth. It was comfortable to be next to her and not need to talk. Then, a feeling settled in his gut. There were only a few more days before he'd need to leave and with the way he was feeling, he wasn't sure he was going to be able to keep pretending they were friends.

They spent the rest of the evening playing all the games over again. Mitchell laughed at the sound of her scream as she beat him, and savored the quiet moments they had waiting in line.

Charlie talked about her childhood. What it was like growing up in such a small community. It boggled his mind. The only person who knew him somewhat personally was his doorman and even then, Mitchell doubted that he'd help him change a flat tire if it wasn't his doorman's job.

They were waiting in line at the churro stand when Charlie glanced over at him. "You're sure quiet." She smiled, and he felt his resolve to stay away from her melt.

He clenched his fists to ground himself and stepped farther away so there was no chance that they would touch. "Just imagining what it was like, growing up in a small community."

She stared out toward the ocean. It stretched out as far as he could see. "It's hard when everyone knows your business. When Alex and I broke up, I couldn't even go grocery shopping without someone talking to me about it."

"Ooo. Ouch." Mitchell sucked his breath in. He could only imagine what that felt like.

Charlie giggled. "That doesn't happen in New York?"

He shook his head. "Naw. It would be weird— I have to admit."

She nodded as she took a step closer to the cashier. He watched as her curly hair fell off her shoulder. It was hard to resist the temptation to run his fingers through it.

"That's what's great about this place. I love having personal relationships with so many people. It really is home." Her voice softened.

Mitchell nodded. A few seconds later, she turned as if she'd expected him to say something, so he smiled at her. "Makes sense. I don't know what that's like, but I understand the draw."

Mitchell ordered two churros and within seconds they were handed to him.

"Thanks," Charlie said. The wrapper crinkled as she took it then she turned and walked away.

She was picking pieces off and slipping them into her mouth when Mitchell fell into step with her. Her skin glowed in the festival lights as she smiled at him. She looked content. He loved the soft lines of her cheekbones and lips. And the way the wind blew, picking up pieces of her hair and swirling them around.

"Well, I should probably get back," she said, glancing up at him.

He never wanted her to go. "How about we listen to some music. After all, isn't that why we're at a music festival?"

She studied him then her gaze fell to the stand where a middle-aged man was grasping the microphone and singing into it.

Mitchell felt her hesitation. "Just a few songs then we'll go. I promise." He brushed her elbow as he took a step forward.

"Okay," she said and followed.

They finished their churros as they headed over to the band-stand. Mitchell found a vacant spot in the grass and motioned for her to sit down. They sat there, staring out at the ocean.

He tried to ignore the tapping of her fingers against her thigh until he could no longer stand it. Not even asking, he grabbed her hand and stood.

"Dance with me," he said, pulling her to her feet.

"Mitchell, I—"

He stared at her. It was a dance. He wasn't spending money on her or pledging his love. The look on his face must have convinced her because she dropped whatever she was going to say and complied. He wrapped his arm around her back and pulled her close. She didn't hesitate.

The song ended and the crowd cheered, but Mitchell kept her close. After the applause died down, the singer began his next song—*When You Love Someone*, by Bryan Adams.

"I love this song," Charlie whispered.

Mitchell tightened his arm around her back and led her into a box step. He loved the feeling of her body so close to his. As much as he wanted to deny it, he trusted her. More than he'd ever trusted Victoria.

She glanced up at him. "Can I ask you something?"

Mitchell closed his eyes and continued dancing to the music. "Sure."

"What happened? You know, with Rose and your family."

His stomach sank like a rock, and he furrowed his brow.

"I'm sorry. It's not my place," she said.

She began to step back and out of his arm, but he wouldn't allow it. Tightening his grip, he opened his eyes. "No. Don't go."

She hesitated then relaxed her body allowing him to pull her close again. "Okay."

Mitchell stared off over her head. "Rose used to take care of me and my brother when my parents were gone building their real estate business. Most weeks, we'd see them for an hour or two and that was it." He dropped his gaze down to meet hers.

"One night, we were at a friend's house to sleep over. My brother, Jimmy, got sick so they called Rose. She'd been out with her lady friends earlier and was exhausted, but she came to pick us up anyway. On the way home, a truck ran a red light and hit us." He swallowed as the memory of the screams and metal crunching raced back to him.

"It's okay, you don't have to keep going," Charlie whispered.

Mitchell shook his head. "I want you to know."

She chewed her lip and nodded.

"The truck hit our car on Jimmy's side. He died instantly."

Her face dropped as she stared at him.

"My parents couldn't forgive her, and they couldn't forgive themselves. They divorced and my dad disappeared. I guess the guilt just ate at him..." Mitchell's voice dropped off as emotions took hold of his throat.

Charlie stopped dancing. Suddenly, she dropped his hand and pulled him into a hug. He wrapped his arms around her back and clung to her. In that moment, Mitchell never wanted to let her go.

15

CHARLIE

*C*harlie swayed to the music as Mitchell kept his arms wrapped around her. What a horrible thing to have happened to his family. Her heart went out to Rose and his parents. And to lose his dad on top of that? Her heart broke for him.

She pulled back and looked up. He met her gaze, and she could feel all the pain and hurt he'd been carrying around for all those years.

"I'm so sorry," she whispered.

His face was solemn as he nodded. "It's okay. It wasn't your fault."

She chewed her lip as she studied his face. Her gaze trailed down to his lips. They were inches from her. If she rose up onto her tippy toes, she just might be able to brush them with hers. And she wanted to do that. Press her lips to his and take away all his pain.

His gaze stayed on her as he leaned down. Apparently, he had the same idea. She took a breath to say something, but instantly forgot words as his lips met hers. They were soft and gentle.

He pulled her against him, and she threaded her fingers through his hair to deepen the kiss. There was so much pain and longing wrapped up in his emotions. She wanted to help him forget.

The sound of a phone chiming broke them apart. Mitchell lowered her to the ground with a sheepish look on his face.

Charlie reached into her purse and pulled out her phone. Her heart sank as she read the text. It was a picture of Alex next to a huge yellow snapper, and he had his thumbs up.

Caught this for you babe cause you're such a catch. I love you and can't wait to spend tomorrow with you.

She glanced over at Mitchell who was standing a few inches from her. What had she done? Here she was complaining about Alex cheating on her and now? She was doing the same thing.

She shoved her phone back into her purse and backed away.

Mitchell's brows furrowed as he watched her retreat. "Hey." He reached out to grab her elbow. "What's wrong?"

She slipped away before he could touch her. "I have to go. I'm sorry. We should have never done that."

Turning, she pushed through the other dancers. She needed some space and some air.

"Charlie. Charlie!" Mitchell called out, but she didn't stop.

Why didn't she just have him drop her off at her car? She was such an idiot. Keeping her head down, she pushed out to the parking lot.

"Charlie?" Priscilla called out.

Relief filled her chest. Turning, she glanced around. When she located Priscilla's waving hand, she veered over to it.

"What's wrong?" Priscilla asked, studying Charlie's face.

"Can you give me a ride to my car?" Charlie could hear Mitchell calling her name.

"Who's calling for you—is that the guy from the diner?"

Charlie gave Priscilla a pleading look. "Please. Can you give me a ride to my car?"

Priscilla looked confused, but nodded. "Okay."

Grabbing her hand, Charlie pulled her from the group of people she was with. "Thanks."

They were at Priscilla's car in a matter of minutes. As she pulled away, Charlie saw Mitchell stop and watch them drive by. Her heart broke as she saw the look on his face. But what could she do? She was an awful, terrible person.

The car was silent. Priscilla turned to her. "Wanna tell me what's going on?"

Charlie watched the trees flash by the window. Clouds had rolled in with the threatening rain. It fit her mood perfectly. "Not really."

"Oh no. You don't get to pull me away from my friends while you have a rich and handsome man following you just to tell me you don't want to talk about it." Priscilla gave her an expectant look.

Charlie knew from that look that she better start talking. "I'll tell you. Just head to my car. It's on Highway Seventy."

Priscilla nodded and turned left. "Deal."

"I was running away from Mitchell because he kissed me."

Priscilla sputtered. "Rich guy kissed you?"

"Can you stop calling him "rich guy"? He has a name. And yes, he kissed me."

Priscilla's hand went out. "Wait. So why did you run? I'd be celebrating."

"Because I'm with Alex now, and Mitchell's engaged to be married."

Priscilla's head whipped around to face Charlie. "What? Since when?"

"Yesterday." Charlie paused. "For both."

"Wow. That was fast."

Charlie chewed her lip. Yeah, it was. In fact, it was the exact thing she had been worried she might do. Jump into a relationship head first. What was she thinking?

"So, you were running from Mitchell because he kissed you, but you're dating Alex now?"

Charlie nodded. "Right."

"And kissing another person was exactly what Alex did to you when he broke your heart."

She nodded again. "Right."

Priscilla pulled onto Highway Seventy. "What are you going to do?"

Charlie wanted crawl into bed and never get out, but that wasn't realistic. "I don't know. It's hard. He's staying with me at the house."

"He's what?" Priscilla's eyebrows shot up.

"Not like that. His grandma is Rose. That's another reason why I'm such a jerk. Rose is finally starting to remember things and feeling motivated to get out of bed. If he called off his wedding for me, she'd be crushed."

Priscilla studied the road as she drove. "You can't live your life hoping Rose might remember you. She wouldn't want that," she said as she pulled over as Charlie's red car came into view.

Charlie let out an exasperated sigh for two reasons. One, because deep down, she knew Priscilla was right. Rose wouldn't want her to halt her life in anticipation of a few fleeting moments that may or may not come. And two, because Gordon Jones, the town's sheriff, was out of his car and circling hers.

"I know. Thanks for the ride. I'll talk to you later," Charlie said as she got out. Priscilla waved and pulled back onto the highway.

"Hey, Gordon," Charlie said as she walked up to him. Thunder rumbled above them as the clouds crept closer.

"Charlie," he said, tipping his hat. "What happened here?"

"Car trouble." It wasn't the truth, but how was she going to explain to this man that she'd run off into the woods, blacked out, and was saved by a handsome, confusing man? Gordon would just look at her like she was crazy. "But it's okay now."

Gordon eyed her. "You can't just leave your car parked on the side of the road. If it's working, you need to move it." He tapped the paper pad he had in his hand with a pen.

"I know. I'm sorry. I had to wait for a ride out here."

He ripped a ticket and handed it over. "Sorry, Charlie. I gotta write you up."

Charlie swallowed and nodded. Yet another bill she owed. They were starting to bury her. "It's okay. I understand."

"You can always fight it," he said as he headed over to his squad car and opened the door.

Charlie nodded. She wouldn't remember to do that. She'd just pay it and get it over with. Gordon got into his car, and she did the same. He pulled away, and she made sure to go in the opposite direction.

Not sure what to do, she drove around the streets. She didn't want to head back home just yet. What if Mitchell was there? Would he want to talk about the kiss?

As she idled at a red light, she brought her fingers to her lips. She could still feel the warmth of his embrace. Butterflies erupted in her stomach as she thought of his hands on her waist, wrapping her up, and taking away all the pain that ached her heart.

A car honked.

Charlie jumped and glanced up. The light was green, so she pressed on the gas pedal and waved to the driver behind her. She needed to get her head on straight and stop allowing Mitchell and his kiss to distract her. There were too many people in her life that would get hurt if she didn't.

After ten minutes of aimlessly driving around, Charlie made her way back to the house. The rain started to fall and splattered against the windshield. She parked the car and got out. Just as she was making her way toward the back door, Mitchell's pink car pulled past.

She fought the urge to sprint up the stairs and hide in her room. Before she could decide what to say to him, he got out of his car and walked straight over to her. There was pain and frustration written all over his face.

"What was that, Charlie?" he said. His voice sounded as if his emotions were choking his throat.

Rain fell on her face and rolled down her cheek. "What?" she asked. Even though she knew what he was talking about. Kisses like theirs only happened in the movies. There was something there, and it frightened her.

"Why did you run away from me? I trusted you." He pushed his hand through his damp hair.

"Mitchell, I..." She stared at the ground. They couldn't continue this. She needed to put a stop to it before she hurt everyone. "We can't do this anymore. You're here to see Rose and getting married will make her happy. Let's not do something we might regret. Please,"—she swallowed— "just leave me alone."

The Adam's apple in his throat rose and fell, and his eyes widened. "But—"

"It's what's best for all of us. Who are we kidding? I'm with Alex, and I love him." The words tasted wrong on her tongue.

The rain fell harder now, drenching her hair, and causing her dress to stick to her legs. She was grateful for it though. The droplets hid the tears that ran down her face. Why was she so sad? This was the right thing to do. She should feel relief. "I'll help you with the wedding, but after that, we're done."

She wrapped her arms around her chest and headed into the house. Glancing behind her, she saw Mitchell standing there, staring at the ground. He hadn't moved. Half of her wanted him to run after her. To scoop her up into his warm arms. The other half was relieved that he stayed where he was. She feared the pain that caring for him would bring. Walking away was the easiest solution.

Once she was inside, she headed to her room and shut the door. The tears came more freely now. Stifling a sob, she pulled off her wet dress and slipped into her fleece pj's. By the time she'd towel dried her hair and threw it up into a bun, her tears had subsided. Her bed beckoned her. Pulling the covers back, she crawled into it.

There was a soft knock on her door. She flipped onto her other side and waited. If it was Mitchell, she didn't want to talk to him.

"Charlie?" Penny's soft voice called from the other side.

"Penny?" she asked, sitting up. "Come in."

Penny pushed the door open and walked in. Charlie must have looked like a mess because Penny's face fell the minute she saw her.

"What happened?" she asked as she crossed the room and sat on the bed.

Charlie contorted her face, trying to stop the tears from starting up again. "I... it's..." Her heart hurt. Her body hurt. She didn't want to think about it anymore.

Penny reached out and grasped her hand. "It's okay. You don't have to tell me right now."

Charlie pinched her lips together and nodded. She was thankful that Penny understood her so well.

They sat in silence while Charlie composed herself. Once the threat of tears subsided, she smiled at Penny.

"How did it go today?" she asked.

Penny stared at her as if there was something she wanted to say. "It went well. Pretty quiet." She pulled her hand away and studied them as they sat in her lap.

"Penny, what happened?"

Penny turned her hands around for a moment before she glanced back to her. "I'll tell you tomorrow. Once you've had a good night's sleep." She reached out to pat Charlie's leg.

Charlie grabbed her hand. "Penny, tell me. What happened?" Her heart raced. Had something happened to Rose? To Francis?

Penny hesitated as she stared at Charlie, then sighed. "The bank called today."

Charlie's stomach plummeted.

"They said the grace period has ended. They're taking the house back at the end of the month." Penny narrowed her eyes as if she were evaluating Charlie's response.

"Oh," was all she could say.

"I told them they must've be mistaken, but from the look on your face...they aren't. Why didn't you tell me it was this bad?"

Charlie stifled a sob. Perhaps, it would have better to discuss this when she had had a night to gain control of her emotions. "I didn't want you guys to worry. I had it under control, but things got away from me."

Penny covered Charlie's hand with hers. "You should have told us. We would've helped. This isn't something you should have to carry on your own. I said it once and I'll say it again, your grandmother never wanted this place to be a burden."

As much as she fought it, a sob emerged. "But she's gone and this place is the only thing left to remind me of her. I can't get rid of it."

Penny studied her. "I know it's hard." She paused as she glanced around the room. "Get some sleep. We'll talk about this in the morning. We can't solve the problem tonight." She shot Charlie a small smile and stood.

Charlie nodded. That sounded like a good idea. Once Penny shut her door, she buried herself under the covers. She'd stay there until her heart stopped breaking.

16

MITCHELL

*M*itchell stood in front of the mirror with a towel wrapped around his waist. He was staring at his reflection through the steam that had built up from his shower. He pressed his fists down on the counter and stared at the faucet. His life was a gigantic mess.

Pinching his lips together, he rolled his shoulders. He'd waited out in the rain for a good ten minutes. Part of him had hoped that Charlie would race from the house and jump into his arms. His heart pounded at the thought of his lips against hers.

It was a kiss like no other. He had borne his soul to her. Told her things he couldn't even tell his friends. Shown a part of himself that he'd hidden deep inside. The look in her eyes had told him everything he needed to know. She cared about him, so he leaned in.

Growling, he pushed down on the countertop and stepped back. He was fighting the thought that he knew was there. He didn't love Victoria. She had never made him feel this way. When he'd told her about his family, she'd grown silent as if she couldn't handle the information and changed the subject.

He scrubbed his stubble and swiped the fog from the mirror. His eyes peered back at him.

"You know what this means, right?" he said to his reflection.

He couldn't say it out loud, but the words pounded in his skull. He was in love with Charlie. Deep, soul kicking love. There was nothing that he wanted more then to wrap her into his arms and take care of her. She saw him for who he really was. Not his money or his status, but for him.

Grabbing his wet clothes, he pulled open the bathroom door and headed into his room. He dressed in his sweats and walked over to the bed. The stupid, lumpy mattress sagged as he sat down. Too worked up to sleep, he stood. He'd had enough of being idle. He needed a job.

Back in the hall, he descended the stairs. At the bottom, he kept his gaze from falling on Charlie's door. As much as he wanted to walk over and knock on it, she'd been clear— there was no way they could be together. It was pointless to hope.

He walked toward the front door. All ten mattresses were stacked on top of each other in the front room. A smile twitched on his lips. He'd found his job.

Grabbing the top mattress, he carried it up to his room. Resting it against his door frame, he walked over to his bed and stripped it of its sheets. Perhaps with a bit more gusto than necessary.

After his mattress was replaced, he brought the old one down, grabbed the next one, and headed up to Victoria's room. His muscles relaxed as he worked. All the tensions that had built up inside of him started to dissipate. With each door, he introduced himself to the resident. They were more than happy to let him in.

Once their mattresses were switched, they shook his hand and he dragged the used one out.

Rose didn't recognize him when he entered. He was grateful for that. At this moment, he didn't know if his heart could handle another round of "who are you?" She smiled at him when he left, and he promised her he would be back tomorrow.

After nine of the ten mattresses were switched, he studied the last one. It was Charlie's. Did he dare? He peered over to her shut door. He picked up and set the mattress down at least five times before he cursed at himself. He was being stupid. If he was going to get over her it needed to start now. He could be her friend.

Yeah, right.

He flexed his hands as he shook his head. No. He could do this. There was no way he'd lose her as a friend. Even if that meant pushing all his feelings down. Before he lost his nerve, he grabbed the mattress and headed to her room. He propped the it up with his knee and knocked.

Silence.

He waited then knocked again.

Seconds ticked by, but then he finally heard movement on the other side. The door opened, and Mitchell sucked in his breathe. Charlie stood there, her hair pulled up into a bun, and her eyes red. She'd been crying.

"Mitchell?" she asked as she wiped her cheeks. "I thought you were Penny."

He swallowed. The uncontrollable desire to take away all of her pain burned in his chest. "Sorry," he said, hoping his voice wouldn't give away his emotions. "Do you mind?" He nodded toward the mattress.

Her face fell as she followed his gesture. "Sure," she whispered.

Stepping back, she pushed the door open. He grabbed the mattress and entered. It was small, like the other rooms, but this was the first room in the whole house that looked as if a younger woman lived there. The furniture was old, but the decorations were updated.

Charlie stripped her bed and then stood in the corner, hugging the comforter and sheets as she watched him. He wanted to ask her if she was okay. He couldn't stand her tear stained face. He hated that there was a chance he was the cause of it.

After he put the new mattress down, Charlie walked over and began replacing the fitted sheet. He couldn't help it. He reached down and tucked the sheet over the corner nearest him. As he pulled on it, it slipped off the side Charlie had just secured.

"Sorry," he mumbled as his face heated.

She shook her head. "It's okay. I've got this." She reached out and replaced her side, but in the process, the corner Mitchell had just put on slipped off.

Grabbing it, he replaced it. This time, with a bit more force. The corner Charlie had just fixed flew off and rested in the middle of the mattress.

"I think your sheet's broken," he said, nodding toward the bed.

Charlie chewed her lip. "I think it's the mattress."

Mitchell humphed. That wasn't it. "It's a good mattress." Why wouldn't she just let him help her? Why did she have to be so tough all the time?

"My other mattress didn't do this."

He glanced over at the lumpy abomination she called a mattress. "That thing is like a hundred years old."

"It is not." She walked over and placed her hand on it. "It's a good mattress. Familiar."

Frustration tingled his spine. "Well, sometimes new isn't bad either. This mattress will be good to you." He sat down on the bed and stared at her.

"I never asked for a new mattress. Maybe I don't want it." She narrowed her eyes.

"Maybe you should give the new mattress a chance. You might like it better."

"Well..." Her gaze moved from the bed up to meet his. "The old mattress is what's best for me right now." Her voice lowered as she studied the floor. "I love the old mattress."

Mitchell had enough of this. She knew very well that this

conversation had nothing to do with the new mattress. "I'm going to bed. I have a big day tomorrow. You know, I'm competing as a lumberjack." He gave her a quick nod and slipped out the door.

Up in his room, Mitchell flopped onto his bed. His mattress held its form as he stretched out across it. He didn't know what Charlie was talking about. The new mattress was awesome.

Grabbing his phone, he turned it on. He'd missed a text from Victoria.

Wrapped things up here. Heading back tonight. Will be there in the morning.

He contemplated texting her back, but knew she was in the air by now. There was no point. Instead, he clicked on the search tab and punched in "lumberjack competitions".

He spent the rest of the evening watching YouTube videos until he fell asleep.

The morning sunlight burst into his window and fell onto his face. He'd spent the last half an hour trying to ignore it. Sighing, he threw off his covers and sat up. No point in trying to keep sleeping. He was actually looking forward to returning to New York where it wasn't light all the time.

Or maybe because Charlie wasn't in New York.

Before he allowed himself to delve into more thoughts about that aggravating woman who slept downstairs, he dressed and brushed his teeth.

As he descended the stairs, laughter carried from the open kitchen door. Curious about who was here, he walked over and peered in.

"Sweetheart!" Victoria exclaimed.

Glancing over, he saw Charlie and Victoria sitting at the table with two coffee mugs in hand. Victoria stood, crossed the room, and practically jumped into his arms. After placing a sloppy kiss on his lips, she pulled away.

"I missed you." She gave him a huge smile.

He fought the urge to push her away. It was way too early in the morning to be dealing with her brand of crazy. He glanced over at Charlie who was staring at her coffee as she made swirls in it with her spoon.

"Did you miss me?" Victoria asked, an expectant look on her face.

"Yeah." He nodded and headed to the counter where he grabbed a mug and filled it. The hot liquid burned his throat, but he needed the pick-me-up it would give, so he downed it fast.

"I got my dress, a caterer, and a photographer. They all thought I was crazy, but then they changed their mind when they heard the amount we were offering." She giggled as she walked back over to the table.

"No need for a caterer, I found one." Mitchell filled his mug again then turned and leaned against the counter.

Charlie had remained quiet as she sat. Why wasn't she talking? He wanted her to say something. He could tell that she was worried. He wished he knew about what.

Victoria sputtered. "Really? Who?"

"The local diner and my new business investment is going to do it."

A high-pitched laugh filled the room. "A diner? Are you serious? Do you know the high-profile people who will be coming?" She dumped some creamer into her coffee and stirred. "Diner? I don't think so. They only serve things fried and slathered in gravy."

Victoria's voice set Mitchell on edge. "Listen, Vic, we're going with the diner. My grandmother remembered it, so we're going to do it."

Her face reddened as she met his gaze. "I don't care who wants this diner to cater, Mitchell. This is my day. I say who feeds us."

Charlie's face fell as she glanced from Victoria over to Mitchell. "Listen, I'll talk to Jorge. I'll let him know he really needs to bring his A-game. Don't fire him. This town could really use the money."

Victoria studied Charlie then sighed. "Fine. But mine is coming as well. In case that man is incompetent."

"Geez, Vic." Mitchell shot her a look, but she just brushed it off.

"So, what are we doing today?" she asked as she sidled up next to him.

The videos of men with chainsaws and axes from the night before raced through his mind. He hadn't realized how difficult it was when he agreed to participate. "I'm competing in a lumber-jack competition."

Victoria brought her mug to her lips and took a sip. "What's that?"

"Where we use chainsaws and such to compete," Mitchell explained.

Victoria shivered. "Ugh. Outside stuff?"

Mitchell nodded. "Yeah. You gonna come?" Inside, he was hoping she'd say no. He wanted to break things off with her, but there was no way he could do that and not disappoint the two women in his life he wanted to please. He was in such a mess, and he wasn't sure how he was going to get out of it.

Two other residents entered, grabbed a plate, and dished up their food. Victoria slunk closer to the edge of the kitchen as she watched them. They said hello to Charlie, who smiled at them, and then they left.

With the room now cleared, Victoria shook her head and neared Mitchell. "I'm not staying here with these old people, so yes, I'm coming."

Mitchell forced a smile. "Great."

The back door opened, and they all turned to see who it was.

Mitchell tried not to groan as Alex walked into the kitchen. His face lit up when he saw Charlie.

"Hey, babe!" he said as he walked over and leaned down.

Mitchell's stomach twisted as Alex kissed her. All the anger he'd felt from the last few days bubbled over. Turning, he focused on the countertop behind him. He fought the urge to run over there and punch the guy. Alex didn't deserve her.

"Ready, Mitchell?" Alex asked.

Mitchell pinched his lips together and turned, nodding as he met Alex's gaze. "Yep."

"We're gonna take my buddy's boat out. The place we practice at is about an hour boat ride away." Alex grabbed Charlie's hand and pulled her to her feet. He wrapped his arm around her waist. "Wear something comfortable."

Mitchell glanced down at his basketball shorts and t-shirt. "Yep."

Victoria giggled as she pressed herself against Mitchell. "This should be interesting."

Charlie avoided his gaze as she passed him on the way out. She smiled over at Alex, and Mitchell's heart sank. He needed to put his feelings aside right now. She wasn't his, and she never will be.

17

CHARLIE

$\mathcal{A}$lex kept his hand on her leg as he drove the four of them to the docks. Charlie fought the urge to push it off. She really didn't like his constant need to touch her right now.

Mitchell and Victoria were surprisingly quiet, which Charlie appreciated. She really wasn't in the mood to talk today. The bank's impending foreclosure loomed over her head like a bad dream.

Once Alex parked, they climbed out, and made their way to a boat titled "Miss Thang". Charlie raised her eyebrows as she nodded toward it.

Alex snorted. "What?"

"Miss Thang?"

He shrugged. "What can I say? My buddy's got a sense of humor."

Alex hopped onto the boat and extended his hand. Charlie grabbed it and he pulled her on. From the corner of her eye, she saw Mitchell do the same to Victoria.

Once they were all on the boat, Alex headed to the wheel and started it up. Charlie took a seat at the back, so she could stare out to the ocean. If she was lucky, she just might see some whales. It was her favorite pastime with her grandmother.

"This seat taken?" Mitchell's voice broke her thoughts.

She turned and cursed herself for looking into his gaze. There was so much that he was saying through it, and she wasn't sure she was ready to process it all. She should have never let herself kiss him. That was a door she could no longer close. How was she going to be around him now?

"Where's Victoria?" Bring up his fiancée. That helped remind her that he wasn't hers.

He glanced behind him as he sat, apparently not waiting for an invitation. "She gets seasick, so wanted to stay at the front."

"Oh." She glanced out to the water as Alex pulled from the dock.

The boat kicked up the water as it sped away. The smell of salt and the feel of the breeze on her face relaxed her. She closed her eyes. This was familiar. Here, there was nothing to worry about.

"Do you do this a lot?"

"Hmm?" she asked, keeping her eyes shut.

"Go on boat rides. It suits you."

She glanced over to Mitchell who was staring at her. Heat raced to her cheeks. "Yeah. It's something I used to do with my grandmother before she passed away. We'd go out searching for whales." She pushed her hands out and stared at her fingers. "Have you ever seen a whale?"

"Like in person?"

She nodded.

"No. Never really had the time."

Charlie eyed him. That was sad. He had all that money, but never took the time to enjoy such a majestic creature.

Mitchell's brows furrowed. "What?"

She shrugged as she turned her focus back to the water. "It's just sad. All that money and you've never seen a whale."

Silence.

"Show me?" he asked, his voice low.

Refusing to look at him, she nodded. "Alex?"

"Yeah?" he asked.

"Got binoculars?"

"Bin right behind you."

Charlie rifled around in old fishing gear and lifejackets until she found them. Then she settled in next to Mitchell. He'd moved closer to her, and she tried to ignore how good he smelled.

"The key to spotting a whale is looking for the blow. That's when the whale reaches the surface of the water and blows out its air." She peered out across the water. "They like to stick close to the shore. That's where fish hang out."

The sound of the boat cutting through the water filled the air as Charlie grew silent. She kept her gaze peeled for the white gush of water.

After about ten minutes, Mitchell spoke up. "Looks like they're not out right now."

She smiled. "It takes patience. Keep looking." Just as she finished the last word, she saw a stream shoot up from the water's surface. "There!" She tried to keep from yelling as she pointed out to the water.

"What?" Mitchell asked.

"Wait for it." She couldn't help it, she held her breath as she waited.

Mitchell leaned closer to her. She turned her head slightly to look at him. His gaze was fixed on the spot she was pointing.

"Are you sure?" he asked with his voice low.

Shivers ran down her spine from his closeness. "Yes," she whispered.

Mitchell grew quiet as he kept his gaze on the water. She wondered if he felt the same. Did his knees turn to Jell-O whenever he got close to her? Was it all in her head? She would move if there was more room on the bench. At least, that's what she told herself.

"No way!" Mitchell yelled as he clapped his hands.

Right where she was pointing, a whale's blow rose up in front of them.

"That's awesome," he exclaimed as he clamped his hand onto her shoulder.

Her body shook from the force. He glanced down at her with a huge smile on his face. His hand lingered as he kept her gaze.

"Thanks," he said with his face inches from hers.

Her stomach knotted. The kiss they'd shared yesterday rushed back to her. In this moment, she wanted to kiss him. Suddenly, Alex and Rose faded away and all she needed was to be wrapped in his arms.

Desperate for a distraction, she shoved the binoculars into his hands. "Here," she said as she pushed off the bench and stood. "It's even cooler if they breach. Keep your eyes out. You won't regret it."

His face fell as he took the binoculars from her. "Are you sure?" His voice grew quiet. "You were here first."

She nodded. Maybe a bit too fast. She forced herself to slow down and smile at him. "I'm fine. You've never seen this before. Go ahead." She stumbled backwards as she made her way over to Alex who was watching them with his eyebrows raised.

Once she was settled on a chair, she kept her gaze on her side of the boat. She feared what would happen if she glanced toward the back. Wrapping her arms around her chest, she closed her eyes. What was happening?

Finally, Alex pulled up to the dock and killed the engine. Charlie was relieved to get off the boat and get some space from Mitchell. They'd seen four whales breach the water and each time, Mitchell cheered and smiled at her. She couldn't help it. Her insides turned to mush every time.

"Ready?" Alex asked as he hopped out of the boat and tied it off.

Charlie nodded and climbed out, not waiting for Alex to help her. She needed air, which was weird since they'd just come from the ocean. As she walked down the dock toward the shore, she glanced around. It'd been a long time since she'd been here. She and Alex used to come to this practice arena every weekend when they were dating. When they broke up, she no longer had a reason.

Six ninety-foot poles rose up from the ground a few hundred feet from the water. A deep pool had been dug for the log rolling and boom run. Alex and his buddies took this competition seriously. As she neared the small cabin that sat in the middle of the practice area, she paused and glanced behind her.

Mitchell was helping Victoria out of the boat. She clung to him for dear life. Once she was off the dock, her face relaxed.

"So, what is all of this?" Charlie heard her ask Alex as they made their way up the shore.

"Back in the day, when logging was done by hand, they used to have these competitions to help ease the monotony of daily life. Now, you can compete all over the world. We basically do things that loggers used to do in the past."

"Which ones are we doing today? The standing block chop? Double buck?" Mitchell asked, glancing over to Alex.

Alex didn't seem impressed. "Looks like someone Googled. We're gonna practice log rolling, the boom run, the double buck, and the standing block chop." He leaned over to Victoria. "We've got a competition coming up."

Two guys stepped out from the cabin and waved Alex over. He nodded and headed in their direction.

"What is he talking about?" Victoria asked Mitchell as they approached.

"Log rolling is where there are two people on a log and they try to spin their competitor into the water," Charlie said as she joined them.

Mitchell glanced over to her. "Yeah, and the boom run is where we'll run head to head across a boom which is basically a chain of logrolling logs."

Victoria scrunched her nose. "Why?"

Mitchell laced his fingers and pressed his hands out. His knuckles popped from the pressure. "It's fun."

"It's barbaric," Victoria scoffed.

"Come on, Mitchell," Alex called, waving his hand for him to follow.

Mitchell nodded and headed in Alex's direction.

Victoria and Charlie walked across the grass and over to a few log seats. "Looks like it's just you and me," Charlie said, hoping to break the awkwardness.

Victoria brushed her hand against the top of the log and sat down. Her face contorted into a look of disgust.

Pleasantries didn't work. Charlie felt uncomfortable sitting next to this woman. Did she suspect that Charlie and Mitchell had kissed yesterday? Or was this just her personality?

"So, you got a dress?" Charlie tried again.

Victoria sighed and nodded. "Yes. It's a Reem Acra." Her eyebrows shot up as if that were impressive.

Charlie had never heard of that person, so just nodded along. "Wow." Was that a guy or a girl? She felt stupid asking, so kept her lips pinched.

"She doesn't normally do wedding dresses in a day, but she did for me."

Ah, it was a girl. "Wow, that's nice."

Victoria grasped her leather purse. The sun glinted off the diamond on her hand. Charlie's stomach fell at the sight. It was Mitchell's ring. He'd given it to her. He wanted to marry her. Charlie needed to remember that.

Voices from behind her drew both of their attention over to

the building. Alex stepped out of the cabin dressed in swim trunks. Charlie smiled. He'd filled out since the last time she'd seen him. He caught her gaze and winked.

Paul and Ralf, his buddies, walked out too. Both wearing trunks.

As soon as Mitchell walked out, Charlie dropped her gaze. She didn't know why she did that. It wasn't like she'd never seen his chest before. But for some reason, she felt uncomfortable.

"Whoo! Doesn't my fiancé look hot?" Victoria exclaimed as she patted Charlie on the back.

Gathering her composure, Charlie looked up. She was acting silly. How was she going to watch them practice with her gaze trained on the ground? As soon as she saw Mitchell, she instantly regretted her decision. In the bright sunlight, she was able to see every chiseled muscle on his body. She could wash laundry on his abs. And he was tan. As if sensing her gaze, Mitchell glanced over at her and a smile twitched on his lips.

Heat raced through her body, so she dropped her gaze. It was probably best if she focused on something else.

"Alright, buddy. Know what to do?" Paul asked Mitchell as they stepped up to a two-foot log that was about fourteen inches in diameter. Paul handed over an axe to Mitchell. "You're going to be competing against Alex, and then we'll switch and Ralf and I will have a go."

Mitchell grabbed the axe and nodded. Alex approached the log next to Mitchell and shot another grin at Charlie.

Paul raised his hand and let it fall as he yelled "Go!"

Charlie tried to keep her gaze from drifting over to Mitchell as he began whacking the log. The muscles in his back tensed with each chop. The sun beat down on his skin that was now glistening with sweat.

She needed to stop staring at his muscles right now. "How long have you known Mitchell?" Charlie turned her attention over to Victoria who had pulled out a file from her purse and was working on her nails. How could she be filing her nails when her fiancé looked so good chopping wood?

"About a year," she said, not looking up. "How about you and Alex? Is that his name?"

Charlie nodded, but when Victoria didn't look up she said, "Yes, it's Alex. And we've kind of been off and on for a while now."

"Hmm," Victoria said.

Charlie sighed and turned back to the guys who were each about halfway through the log. Why did this part have to last this long? Keeping her gaze concentrated on Alex, she decided now would be a good time to start listing all the reason she should be with him. Before her gaze drifted back over to the hunky, bare-chested billionaire.

18

MITCHELL

*M*itchell's muscles burned as he continued chopping the log in front of him. Alex's strikes reverberated in his ears, pushing him to work harder.

Mitchell's workouts at the gym were nothing like this. Sweat rolled down his back as the sun beat down on him.

"And he's done!" Paul yelled out.

Glancing down, Mitchell realized that it wasn't his log that Paul was talking about. Cursing under his breath, he glanced over. The top half of Alex's log had split and was resting next to the bottom.

Alex grinned over at him. "Good work," he said. "Looks like the better man won." He rested the ax on a log and walked over to Charlie. She looked shocked as he pulled her up and dipped her, smacking a kiss right on her lips.

A twinge of anger raced up Mitchell's spine. What was that? Did Alex know? A fire burned in Mitchell's stomach. He wasn't going to let Alex win the next one. He'd make sure of it.

Paul and Ralf set up the logs for themselves, and Alex yelled go. Both men began chopping, so Mitchell took this time to focus. The next competition was the boom run. He glanced over to the pool and studied the logs. He'd win this one. After all, he'd run track in high school.

In a matter of minutes, Alex declared Ralf the winner. Once the axes were cleaned up and the wood discarded, they all made their way over to the pool.

"Want us to go first to show you?" Paul asked.

"Yeah. That'd be good. Then you'll have no one to blame but yourself when you lose." Alex grinned at him.

Mitchell fought the urge to punch him. "That's okay. I think I got it."

"You need to run across the logs, circle that orange cone, then run back. First person to touch the starting spot wins," Ralf said, waving his hand toward the booms. "Don't worry. We heat the pool so you won't freeze if you fall off."

Mitchell walked over until he was lined up with the logs. He glanced over at Alex who was smiling and waving at Charlie.

Mitchell swallowed down his frustration. "Ready?" he asked.

Alex raised his eyebrows as he moved to his starting point. "Jealous?"

They leaned over, resting a hand on their knee.

"Jealous? Of you?" Mitchell snorted. That was a joke. Charlie didn't love Alex. That was obvious. She was just scared and scared was something Mitchell could work with.

"She's mine," Alex said, his voice low.

"We'll see," Mitchell replied just as Paul raised his hand and shouted "Go!"

Mitchell leapt out onto the log. It bowed under his weight. Just as he lifted his foot up, the log began to roll. He had to keep his arms outstretched so he didn't lose his balance. Out of the corner of his eye, he saw Alex shoot past. Frustration built up in his chest, and he quickened his pace.

He raced down the seven booms, jumped onto the platform, and around the cone. The logs had been disturbed and were no longer in a straight line. Instead, they were shifting as the water moved. Mitchell kept his gaze on them as he ran and leapt from each one.

"Mitchell's the winner!" Paul yelled as Mitchell jumped from the last boom and onto the platform.

Once he was on solid ground, he looked around for Alex. Next to the log closet to him was Alex's bobbing head.

Charlie stood next to the edge of the pool. "You okay?" she called out to him as he swam to the platform.

"Yeah, I am," Alex said as he pulled himself from the water.

Inside, Mitchell had hoped she would be cheering for him, but Alex's fall into the water seemed to have her distracted. He tried to force a smile even though this whole competition thing wasn't really giving him the edge he'd hoped it would.

Charlie rounded the pool with a towel in hand. She walked over to Alex who was rubbing the water out of his hair. She spoke softly to him. Mitchell couldn't hear what she was saying.

Desperate for a distraction, he glanced around to locate Victoria. She was sitting on a log with her phone raised. As always, she was too wrapped up in herself to notice anything going on around her. So much for the cheerleader fiancée.

Charlie returned to her seat, and Paul and Ralf lined up in front of the booms. Alex called go, and they sprinted across. Mitchell focused on the next game— the double buck.

When Ralf jumped onto the platform, Alex declared him the winner, and the two high fived.

Mitchell was anxious to get moving. His adrenaline was pumping. He was ready to waste Alex again. "Ready?" he asked, nodding his head toward Alex.

Alex nodded. "Yep." He threw the towel onto the nearby bench and walked over to two white pine logs that were propped up on a platform.

"Hey, Charlie, want to come ref?" Alex asked as he waved his hand and beckoned her over.

Her gaze fell on Mitchell's face as she hesitated. It dropped as soon as he met it with as much intensity as he could muster. Why was she with this guy? He clenched his jaw. How much longer was he going to allow himself to care?

She walked over, and he noticed she kept a significant distance from him. He smiled inside. The closeness he'd felt while on the boat with her was hard to miss. His stomach flipped at the thought. He fought the urge to reach out and pull her close.

"It's me and Mitchell against Paul and Ralf," Alex said as he walked over to a chest and pulled out a giant saw.

"You and me? Together?" Mitchell wasn't sure how he felt about having to work as a team with this guy.

"Yep," Paul said as he lifted a saw out as well.

Alex handed the saw to Mitchell and walked over to Charlie. "Give me a good luck kiss, huh?" He leaned over.

Charlie's face reddened as she studied him. Then she leaned over and kissed him on the cheek. Mitchell dropped his gaze and clenched his hands as he twisted them on the handle of the saw. When he glanced back over to her, she was watching him.

He shot her a smile, but she dropped her gaze to the ground.

"Awe. You will always be my good luck charm." Alex reached down and grabbed the other handle on the saw. "Where's yours?" he asked Mitchell, nodding toward Victoria who hadn't moved from her spot. Together they lifted the saw until the teeth rested on top of the log. "Bored with you already?" he whispered, narrowing his eyes at Mitchell.

Charlie had taken ten steps back, so Mitchell glared at him. "I don't know why Charlie's with you. You don't deserve her."

Alex clenched his jaw. "And you do? You have no idea what you're talking about."

Mitchell staggered his stance as he readied his body. "I do, and she's ten times what you are. I'm going to help her see that."

Alex readied his stance as well. "We have a history. She'll always be there. Some things never change."

Rage raced through his body. Alex was such a jerk. He was leading her on. Was this a competition for him?

Charlie raised her hand, but Alex shook his head to stop her. "Wanna make it interesting?" He asked as he glanced over to Mitchell.

Charlie furrowed her brow. "What?"

"This guy seems to think he has a chance with you."

Mitchell gripped the handle as the desire to deck this guy raced through his body.

Charlie sputtered and glanced over at Victoria who wasn't paying attention to anything but her phone. "Excuse me? He's engaged."

Alex shrugged. "Doesn't matter. He's got feelings for you."

It was true, and Mitchell wasn't ashamed of it. Plus, he wasn't going to let this guy get his goat. "What do you want, Alex?"

A slow smile spread across his lips. "Let's make it interesting. If you win the most games, then you get Charlie. If I win, you back off and leave us alone."

"What?" Charlie raised her voice as she glanced back and forth. "I'm not a prize."

Alex glanced at Charlie then back to Mitchell. "In fact, I'm feeling generous. If we tie, I'll let you take the win."

"If I win, you leave her alone. For good." Mitchell leaned forward and narrowed his eyes.

Alex extended his hand. "Deal."

Mitchell met his gesture.

"I don't want anything to do with this," Charlie said as she stepped back.

"Fine. We'll have Mitchell's date do it. Hey, sweetie?" Alex yelled in Victoria's direction.

She lowered her phone as she stared at him. "Are you talking to me?"

Alex nodded. "Care to ref?"

She swatted her hand around as a bug zeroed in on her. She let out a shriek and jumped from her seat. "Fine. If it gets us back to civilization faster."

"You join Paul, and Ralf'll join me. Can't very well be competing on the same team."

Mitchell nodded. He glanced over to Charlie whose hands were on her hips.

Soon, all four men were set up. Victoria raised her arm and yelled go.

Mitchell threw everything he had into sawing. Thankfully, Ralf was pretty fit and soon they fell into a groove. In no time, they were halfway through. Then three-quarters.

"Winner!" Victoria yelled out.

Mitchell whipped around. Alex was grinning as he held up the piece they'd just removed.

"That's two for me. And one for you," Alex said as he laughed and flung the wood into the stack a few feet away.

Mitchell growled and pulled the saw from the log. "Next." He was ready to get this creep as far away from Charlie as possible.

"The last one we're practicing today is log rolling. You go out into the pool on a log and try to roll each other off of it. You go three times. Each time counts as a win or lose," Paul said as they made their way over to the pool.

Mitchell nodded. Good. Now he could inflict some pain on this guy and not get judged for it. "Perfect." He neared the pool and crouched down, dipping his hand into the water. He cupped his hand and dumped the water over his hair. It cooled his body.

He glanced up to see Charlie walking toward him. She had a sour look on her face. He straightened, bracing himself.

"What are you doing? Are you serious? Competing for me?" She stood there with her hands on her hips.

Mitchell sighed. "I'm doing this for you." Why couldn't she understand that this guy was no good.

"What about what I want? I told you already, I don't need you to do me any favors. I can take care of myself." She folded her arms and narrowed her eyes.

Mitchell scrubbed the stubble on his jaw. Before he could answer, Alex walked up.

"Ready?" Alex asked.

Mitchell nodded then shrugged at Charlie. "I've got to do this."

She narrowed her eyes and stalked off.

He sighed. She'd thank him once that creep was far away from her.

Paul walked over to him. "Here's a pair of birling shoes. They have spikes in them to help." Mitchell took them. As he slipped them on, Paul continued. "Keep your eyes on his feet at all times."

Mitchell nodded as he walked over to a log that Ralf was steadying with a pole. Alex joined him and together they stepped onto the log.

"We good?" Ralf asked.

Mitchell kept his hands out to steady himself. "I'm good."

"Me too," Alex said.

Ralf pushed the log until it was in the center of the pool. Mitchell twisted to keep himself steady.

Once the log stilled, Ralf yelled, "Throw your poles!"

Alex began running on the log. Mitchell wasn't ready and slipped and fell into the water. When he surfaced, he met Alex's mocking gaze.

"Come on, you're not even making this hard." He laughed as he dove into the water and brought the log over to the pool's edge.

Cursing, Mitchell swam over. What was with him? How'd he fall so easily? He pulled himself from the water and walked over to where Alex was standing next to Ralf.

"You have to watch his feet, Mitchell," Paul said as he steadied the log.

Nodding, Mitchell gathered his nerves and stepped back onto the log. He wasn't going to let this jerk win.

Once Alex was situated, Ralf pushed them into the middle of the pool again.

"Throw your poles!" Ralf yelled, and this time Mitchell was ready.

Instead of getting dumped into the pool, Mitchell stared at Alex's feet. When Alex spun one direction, Mitchell changed his. And vice versa.

"You think you're gonna to win her?" Alex's voice cut through Mitchell's concentration.

"That's up to her. I'm just going to get you away," Mitchell replied as he changed direction. Alex faltered for a moment, but steadied himself.

"And then what? You're gonna get married and leave her. This is a tiny island. She knows everyone here."

Mitchell's heart hurt. He didn't want to marry Victoria, but he was pretty sure that Charlie wasn't interested in him either. His life had become such a giant mess. He shrugged. "She'll meet someone. A man who treats her well."

Before Alex could say anything, Mitchell changed direction and Alex fell backwards into the water. Feeling triumphant, Mitchell grinned and slipped in after him. That was one to one. He had one more to win and then Charlie would be free.

19

CHARLIE

*T*his was the most cave-man-like thing any guy had ever done for her. Competing to win her? What was she? A prize? She humphed and kept pacing as she tried to ignore the splashes of water going on next to her.

"That's one for Mitchell, and one for Alex," Paul called out.

Anger boiled over as she gnawed her fingernail. If either guy thought she was leaving with them, they had another thing coming. And why had Mitchell agreed to this? It didn't seem like him. Maybe she didn't know him as well as she thought.

What about Victoria? She glanced over to see Mitchell's fiancée had returned to the logs and was back on her phone. She seemed completely oblivious to the despicable display of testosterone Charlie had ever witnessed. Why did Mitchell take that bet?

Curiosity won over, and she turned to see what was happening. Mitchell and Alex had been pushed back out into the pool and were staring at each other's feet. The log would spin in one direction then in the other.

She allowed herself to think about what it might feel like if

Paul called Alex's name. Anger and pain shot through her body. Maybe she didn't have the feelings for him that she thought she did.

Her gaze landed on Mitchell. His brows were furrowed, and his jaw set as he studied Alex's feet. What would she do if Paul called his name? Anger and annoyance coursed through her.

Rolling her eyes, she folded her arms. Well, that didn't help.

Her breath caught in her throat as Mitchell teetered on the log for a second. A look of triumph flooded Alex's face. But just in time, Mitchell righted himself and jostled the log. Alex waved his arms as he was dumped into the pool.

Mitchell pumped both fists into the air and then disappeared underneath the water's surface.

It was a tie which meant Mitchell had won. Great.

They both exited the water. Alex's face was red as he barreled over to his towel and wrapped it around his waist. Mitchell looked pretty proud of himself as he followed.

Charlie gritted her teeth and stomped over.

"I hope you don't think you really won me," she growled.

Mitchell ran his hand through his hair, spraying water droplets onto the ground. He raised his eyebrows as he studied her. "But, I won."

Heat raced up her spine and burned her cheeks. "Yeah, but I'm not some prize."

He grabbed each end of the towel and rubbed it against his back. "Are you sure? Legally—"

She clenched her jaw and turned. She hated the annoying half smile that was playing on his lips.

His wet hand engulfed her elbow, and he pulled her back. "I know I didn't win you. I was trying to protect you." His voice had grown gruff.

She glanced over. His eyes were sky blue. They were earnest as they searched hers. She swallowed. "I don't need protection," she said as she pulled from his grasp and stomped off.

"Hey!" Alex called after her as she passed him.

"Not now, Alex," she said as she waved him away. All she wanted to do right now was get back home. Back to the place that made sense.

She plopped down next to Victoria who didn't even notice she'd returned. Pulling at the hem of her shirt, she calmed her nerves. Why did Mitchell have to be so sincere when he had talked to her? Why did he have to turn her insides to mush every time he neared?

And why did he want to take care of her? She allowed her gaze to fall on his retreating frame. The men were heading into the cabin to change.

When they returned, Mitchell was talking on his phone. Alex walked up to her and tried to put his arm around her waist. She turned and twisted to dodge him.

"Hey," he complained.

"Take me home," she said as she headed to the dock and climbed onto the boat.

She watched as Mitchell walked over to Victoria. They spoke for a few minutes. Then they made their way to the boat followed by Alex who jumped in, but Mitchell remained on the dock.

"The company we are going to rent the boat through has one of their yachts coming this way. They're going to pick us up so we can see it," Mitchell said as his gaze fell to her.

Charlie shrugged. Why should she care? "Sounds good. That makes sense."

Mitchell's jaw tightened. "Okay. Well, I'll see you later."

Alex nodded and started up the boat. As he pulled away from the dock, Charlie's gaze fell to Mitchell's. A look of confusion and pain filled his eyes the further she got.

What was she supposed to do? Run after him? Throw her arms around him and tell him that she loved him? Her heart sank. What was that? Swallowing, she glanced back at his now tiny frame.

Did she love him? Rubbing her hand over her face, she studied the water. Her heart swelled as she thought about his piercing blue eyes. How kind he'd been to her and the other residents at the house. How he really did want to protect her and take care of her.

She glanced over at Alex whose jaw was set as he focused on the water. Had Alex ever done anything even remotely close to what Mitchell had done? He came and went as he pleased. It was almost as if he was confident she'd never go anywhere.

He could do the most despicable act, and she'd forgive him. And she had. The memory of him locked in a passionate embrace with another woman raced through her mind. Why was she such a fool? How could she have allowed herself to trust him again?

She'd been such an idiot. She pulled her feet up onto the bench and wrapped her arms around her chest. In terms of Mitchell, she didn't know what she thought. But at this moment, all she knew was she and Alex were done.

Alex pulled up to the dock and killed the engine. Charlie stood as he jumped out and tied the boat to a pole. He reached out his hand to help her, but she brushed it off.

She stepped onto the dock and took a deep breath, then turned. "We're done," she said.

Alex's brows shot up. "What?"

She waved her hand between them. "You and me. We're done. Leave me alone."

His mouth hung open as she made her way down the dock. Relief and joy filled her chest. It felt good dumping the baggage he came with.

Twenty minutes later, she opened the back door to the house and the smell of steak and potatoes wafted out. She smiled. This was home. This was where she belonged. Every resident here cared about her and she cared about them.

Penny was standing next to the stove, moving potatoes around on a pan. She smiled when she saw Charlie. "Hey, sweetie. Have fun?"

Charlie nodded and slipped off her shoes. "It was interesting."

Penny peered behind her. "Where's Alex?"

Charlie plopped down on the chair next to the table. "I dumped him."

Penny snorted. "Again?"

"Yep," Charlie said, emphasizing the "p".

Penny placed some food down in front of her. "Good. I never liked that boy."

"You what? Why didn't you tell me?" Charlie traced her finger around the edge of the plate.

"Would you have listened to me if I'd told you that he wasn't good enough for you?" Penny set two more place settings.

Charlie snorted. Probably not. Nodding to the extra plate she asked, "Who's eating with us?"

"Isn't Mitchell?"

Charlie's stomach flipped at the mention of his name. She pinched her lips together and shook her head.

Penny laughed. "You got rid of two guys in one day? What happened?"

Scoffing, Charlie leaned back. "He's boat rental shopping with his fiancée."

"Oh," Penny said as she picked up the plate and placed it into the cupboard.

Silence filled the air.

"Have you decided when you're going to tell the residents? About the foreclosure?" Penny's question drove daggers into Charlie's heart.

She'd forgotten about that. What was she going to do? Not knowing what to say, she fiddled with her fork. "I'm not sure. I can't lose this place, Pen. Granny would be so mad." Tears brimmed her eyes.

A soft hand rested on her shoulder. "Charlie, it's okay. If you have to give this place up— it's okay. It should have never been your job to take care of it. Your granny would want you to be happy and not stressed."

All Charlie could do was nod. She understood the words, but deep down, she felt like a failure.

"Rose, what are you doing out of bed?" Penny asked, stopping to stare above Charlie's head.

Whipping around, Charlie saw Rose standing in the door frame with a scared look on her face. Charlie was out of her chair in an instant. "Rose, what's wrong?"

Rose's pale face peered up into Charlie's. "Tyler. Where is he? Why isn't he here?"

Charlie reached out and grabbed her hand. Anything to help her feel better. "He went out, but he's coming back."

Rose pinched her lips and shook her head. "No. No he isn't. He hates me. I knew he'd leave. He never wanted me at the wedding."

Wrapping her hand around Rose's elbow, Charlie led her into the kitchen. "You remembered? The wedding?" How was that possible? It'd been so long since they'd talked to her about it. For a moment Charlie allowed herself to hope that Rose was returning.

"How could a mother forget her only son's wedding?" Rose sat on the chair that Charlie had pulled out. "But he's gone now, and I'm alone."

Taking both of Rose's hands in hers, Charlie sat and leaned close to her. "I promise you that he's not gone. He's out with his fiancée picking a boat for the reception. He'll be home soon."

Rose's worried gaze met hers. "You promise? He'll come back, and I'll go to his wedding?"

Charlie pinched her lips together. "Yes. I promise. I will do everything I can so you can see your son get married."

A smiled spread across Rose's lips. "Thank you." Then her brow furrowed. "What's your name?"

Charlie swallowed and leaned back. "Charlie."

Her stomach knotted as she thought back to her earlier revelation. It didn't matter if she had feelings for Mitchell or not. What mattered was making Rose happy. She was already failing her grandma, and she couldn't fail Rose as well.

20

MITCHELL

"Good evening, sir," the uniformed man said as Victoria and Mitchell stepped onto the deck of the boat.

Mitchell reached out and shook his hand. "Thanks for accommodating us," he said.

"Absolutely. No problem. We're happy to have you. My name is Terrence, and I'm the reservation specialist for this boat." Terrence nodded his head as he clutched a clipboard in his hand.

A different man stepped up and gated the entrance that they had just passed through. Once it was secure, he waved toward the upper deck and then disappeared.

"It says here that you are looking to get married on Tuesday?" He pulled the board from his chest and peered down at it.

The boat left the dock, and Mitchell's throat went dry. It wasn't what he wanted. He had feelings for Charlie. Deep feelings. But she'd pretty much made it clear that she wasn't interested in him. Instead of speaking, Mitchell just nodded.

Victoria started in, asking questions about champagne and boat capacity. Losing interest fast, Mitchell made his way over to the railing and stared out at the water. It churned as the boat sliced through it.

Allowing his gaze to move farther across the ocean, his heart caught in his throat. He spotted a blow about fifteen feet from the boat. Only moments later, a second, smaller blow shot up from the water. It must be a mom and her baby.

Smiling, he rested his arms on the railing and watched. They kept up with the boat as they methodically rose out of the water to breathe. Mitchell couldn't help it as his thoughts turned to Charlie. How excited she'd been to show him the whales earlier.

Everything about her intoxicated him and drew him in. He swallowed. He knew the answer to Terrence's question earlier. He didn't want the wedding on Tuesday. He didn't want the wedding at all.

A figure drew his attention to his left. Victoria stood next to him with a disgruntled look on her face.

Mitchell furrowed his brow. "Everything okay?"

She sighed and folded her arms. "I'm not sure. This isn't what I've dreamed of my whole life."

He studied her. "Do you love me?"

She stared at him with her eyebrows raised. "What?"

"Love me. Do you love me?" he repeated.

She giggled and rested against the railing. "Of course."

Mitchell leaned in. "Really? This isn't you." He waved his arms around the boat. "My grandmother certainly isn't you."

Her nose crinkled as she nodded.

"Rose is only going to get worse, and I'm going to need to spend more and more time here. Is that something you can do?"

Her face paled. "Here? Come back?"

He nodded.

She sighed and the silence surrounded them. Finally, she pushed back, shaking her head. "No. I don't want this."

Relief filled his chest. "Really?"

She bit her lip and nodded. "Yes. I'm Coach purses and Gucci shoes. I'm not old people and dilapidated houses."

Mitchell patted her arm. "I know."

She began wiggling the ring off her finger. Once it was off, she pushed it onto the finger of her other hand. "Thanks for understanding."

Mitchell nodded.

They rode the rest of the way back to Sitka in silence. As they neared the dock, Mitchell's heart began to pound. He was no longer tied down. Seeing Charlie meant so much more now. What would she say?

"I'm just going to head to the airport and go home," Victoria said after they stepped onto the dock.

Mitchell nodded. "Have a safe flight." He leaned in and kissed her cheek.

She smiled. "Have a nice life." Then headed down the dock with her phone out.

Mitchell started the path back to Dottie's Retirement Home. Thoughts flooded his mind. What a strange couple of days. He'd gone from dating to engaged to single. And all for what?

Charlie.

That thought caused his gait to quicken. He couldn't wait to see her and tell her that the wedding was off. Would she be happy?

He couldn't have been the only one who felt the sparks between them. Even when she was mad at him, she was still the most caring woman he'd ever known.

And he wanted to spend the rest of his life with her.

It felt achingly slow, but finally the retirement home came into view. He neared the back porch to find Charlie sitting in a rocker with her arms wrapped around her chest. His head felt dizzy as he climbed the steps.

"Hey," he said, praying it would come out normal.

His stomach fell when she raised her head and he saw her tear stained face. He leaned over and inched closer. "What's wrong?"

She pinched her lips and shook her head as she turned her gaze toward the parking lot. "Nothing," she whispered.

He grabbed a rocker and pulled it up next to her. "This doesn't look like nothing. Tell me what's wrong."

She turned her gaze back for a moment then glanced around. "Where's Victoria?"

Mitchell leaned back in the chair. "She's on a plane home right now."

"More shopping?"

He turned to look at her. "She's not coming back."

Charlie's face paled. "What? Why?"

He studied his hands. "Because we're not getting married."

Silence.

Curiosity got the better of him, so he glanced over at her. Her lips were pinched as she stared at him.

"What?" she asked.

"There's not going to be a wedding. We're not getting married." There was no reaction on her face. His confession wasn't going as he'd planned.

Charlie stood and walked over to the railing of the porch. "Why? Why would you do that?"

Mitchell stared at her. She couldn't be serious. She had to know. He stood and made his way over to her. "Because I don't love her."

A tear slid down her face. "No. You can't do that. It will break Rose's heart."

"She'll understand." He reached out to touch her arm.

She hugged her chest and turned. "No. She won't. She'll be crushed. This was the last thing that I was going to be able to do for her, and you ruined it."

He couldn't believe what he was hearing. "I think I know Rose more than you do. She wouldn't want me to get married if I don't love the woman."

Charlie whipped around with rage in her gaze. "Know her more than me? Are you serious? She's been here most of my life, and I was there with her through everything. I was the one who watched as she got sicker and sicker." A sob escaped her lips as the tears flowed.

Mitchell's heart hurt. He wanted to wrap her up and take away all her pain. He stepped forward.

"No. Go," she whispered.

"What?"

"Go!" She pointed toward the parking lot.

"You want me to go?" Was he hearing her right?

"Yes. Go before you hurt her more. She was looking forward to the wedding. She was so worried you'd cancel it or have it without her. Go, before you give her more false hope." She dropped her gaze and turned so her back was to him.

Mitchell's stomach plummeted to the ground. He couldn't process the words she was saying. How had things gone so badly so fast? He loved Charlie. She needed to know that.

"But, I—"

"Go." Her shoulders slumped as she kept her back to him. "Please."

His head pounded. He opened his mouth to say something, but as he took in her frail posture, he stopped. She was hurting, and he didn't want to cause her anymore pain.

"I'm sorry," he whispered and headed into the house. The only thing he could think of right now was getting out of this place.

Up in his room, he threw all his clothes into his suitcase. Once he zipped it, he glanced around. Sitting on the chair next to his dresser was the polar bear he'd won for Charlie. He couldn't take it with him. It would be a constant reminder of the woman he couldn't have.

He placed it on the bed and grabbed a piece of paper and a pen. On it he sprawled:

To Charlie. I hope you can forgive me one day.

He tucked the note under the bear, opened his door, and

headed to Rose's room. She was asleep on her bed, so he just leaned over and gave her a kiss.

"Bye, Rose," he whispered. "I'll be back soon."

She stirred, but didn't wake.

By the time he got outside, Charlie was gone. He kept his gaze focused on the bubble gum colored car and threw his luggage onto the backseat. Grabbing his phone, he called Pedro.

"I'm coming. Be ready for me," he said as he started up his car.

"You got it, boss," Pedro said.

Mitchell gunned the gas and peeled out of the parking lot. His mind swam from all the emotions that raced through him. As he pulled up to a red light, he peered out the window.

A flower shop greeted him. Suddenly, he flipped on his blinker and pulled into the lot. An elderly woman stood outside, watering plants.

Her lips parted as Mitchell barreled past her and into the store. "S-Sir, can I help you?"

He glanced around at glass enclosures that held a variety of flower arrangements. "I need some daisies."

"Bouquet or plants?"

"Plants."

She nodded as she waved him back outside. "I have some out here." She motioned toward the plants she had been watering.

"And a shovel. Do you sell those?"

"Well, actually, I don't sell those." Her eyes narrowed as she looked him over. "I guess you can just take mine."

"Really?"

She nodded. "You look like a man on a mission. I'd hate to be the person who got in your way."

Mitchell reached into his pocket and pulled out his wallet. "Thank you." He grabbed out a hundred-dollar bill. The left-over one that Alex didn't get to.

The woman shook her head. "That's okay."

Mitchell leaned in. "You sure?"

"I'm sure." She smiled in a way that reminded him of Rose.

"Thank you." Grabbing the flowers and shovel she held out, Mitchell placed them in the front seat and climbed in. Once the car was started, he pulled out, and headed back down the street.

There was one thing he was going to do before he left, and there was no way Charlie could stop him.

Thankfully, it was easy for him to find his way back to the cemetery, and he was there in under ten minutes. Grabbing the flowers and shovel, he made his way over to the headstone that Francis had stood in front of the day before. The pots next to the stone were still empty.

He pushed the shovel in and removed the dirt until he'd made a big enough hole. He removed the flowers from the container and gave them a good shake. This was the first time he'd ever planted. He hoped he was doing it right.

Once the roots were covered, he took a step back. He hadn't noticed the dark clouds roll in until a drop of rain fell on his face. Glancing up, he welcomed it. The color of the clouds matched his mood.

When the other planter was filled, Mitchell rested his hand on the stone.

"Good to meet you," he muttered before he grabbed the shovel and containers and made his way back to his car. Once inside, he headed to the airport.

Pedro was sitting in the cockpit when Mitchell boarded. He raised his eyebrows as he glanced down at Mitchell's dirty hands.

"Everything okay, boss?"

Mitchell swallowed down his emotions. "Just get me home."

Pedro nodded. "Cops aren't going to be speeding up on me, are they?"

Mitchell shook his head.

A look of understanding fell over Pedro's face. "Woman troubles? You've got that look. Same one my cousin had when his lady left him." He let out a low whistle. "Got his heart broken."

Mitchell washed up in the bathroom then headed to his recliner. "Pedro, just take me home."

Pedro raised his hands and nodded. "No problem. We'll be back home with Alaska behind us in about eight hours."

Mitchell nodded and closed his eyes. Right now, distance was all he wanted.

21

CHARLIE

*C*harlie went to bed with a stomachache. She told herself it was because she'd forgone dinner, but the nagging voice in her head told her that that was a lie. When she woke up the next morning, she found it impossible to get out of bed.

Flipping to her side, she pulled out her phone. She'd missed a call and there was a voicemail. Her heart soared. Was it Mitchell? She couldn't believe what she'd said to him yesterday, but seeing Rose upset had set her on edge.

Unlocking her phone, she sucked in her breath, but the call had been from Jorge. She clicked on the voicemail and turned the speaker on.

Laying back on her pillow, she listened to his familiar, deep accent.

"Listen, Charlie, I know we talked about you coming back, and I'm more than happy to do that. It's just, right now, with my new investor, I'm going to be gutting the diner. So, it'll be closed for the next month. See you once it's over!"

Charlie groaned and shut off her phone. One whole month with nothing to do. She buried her face in the pillow. Well, not nothing. She still needed to tell all the residents that the doors were closing, and they needed to find another place to live.

Too heartbroken to get up, Charlie pulled the blankets back over her head and fell asleep.

∾

"Charlie?" a soft voice called.

She moaned.

"Charlie," it called again. More forcefully this time.

Sitting up, Charlie glanced around. The sun was no longer high in the sky, and it was now casting a bright glow into her room. That voice— she'd know it anywhere. "Rose?"

The familiar smile greeted her. Rose was sitting on her bed with her hands in her lap.

Charlie threw her arms around her. "You're back."

Rose nodded.

Tears ran down her cheeks as Charlie pulled back just to make sure what she saw was true. Rose remembered. "It's been so long," Charlie said through sobs.

Rose nodded and grabbed Charlie's hands in hers. "I know. I'm so sorry."

Charlie shook her head. "No. It's not your fault." Then she waved her hand. "Let's not waste time talking about the past."

Rose stood. "Get dressed. We're having cookies in the kitchen."

Flinging the covers off her body, Charlie nodded. She was in the kitchen in under two minutes. She was pretty sure her shirt was on backwards, but she didn't care. She wasn't going to waste any time.

Floyd was sitting at the table with Rose's hand grasped in his. He had a goofy grin plastered on his face. Charlie took the seat across from Rose, and Penny sat next to her.

They all stared at Rose.

"Okay, someone needs to say something." Rose shot them a smile.

Charlie's heart soared. This was all so familiar, and she never wanted it to end.

"Charlie, let's start with you. Tell me what's happening in your life."

Biting her lip, Charlie shook her head. That was the last thing she wanted to do.

"She just broke up with Alex," Penny offered.

Rose furrowed her brow. "Good. I never liked that kid."

Charlie scoffed. Why hadn't anyone told her?

Rose reached over and grabbed Charlie's hand. "Anyone piqued your interest?"

Mitchell's face flooded Charlie's mind. "Not really."

Penny and Floyd gave her a skeptical look.

"There was someone, but I ran him off." How could she tell Rose that she'd fallen for her grandson, but then broke his heart?

Silence filled the room.

"Will someone say something?" Rose asked, as she glanced from person to person.

"Your grandson came," Floyd said.

Rose's face paled. "Mitchell?"

Penny nodded. "He had no idea where you were. He came as soon as he got the message that you'd gotten sicker."

Rose pushed her chair from the table. "Is he here?"

Penny glanced at Floyd. "I haven't seen him. Charlie, do you know where he is?"

Charlie chewed her bottom lip.

There was a collective sigh around the table.

"What?" she asked.

"You're chewing your lip which means you're nervous. What happened?" Penny asked.

Might as well tell them. "Mitchell left."

Rose furrowed her brow. "What? Why?"

"Because... I chased him away," Charlie whispered.

More silence.

"You love him," Rose said.

Charlie's stomach flipped. "What?"

She dropped Floyd's hand and grasped Charlie's with both of hers. "Honey, it's written all over your face. Tell me what happened."

Charlie took a deep breath and started. She told them all about the first night he was here. How they had danced in the kitchen and almost kissed. How Victoria had come in and stopped them. She told them about how excited Rose had been that he was back, and how she was starting to remember things.

Charlie told them about Alex and the carnival. How Mitchell had confided in her about the past. How they had kissed. And she told them that he tried to say he loved her. But she was too upset about him breaking off the wedding that she ran him out of town.

Finally, she glanced up. Rose had a smile on her face.

"What?" This wasn't the reaction Charlie had expected from someone who had just been told that their estranged grandson left because of a girl.

"Honey, you've got to stop doing that," Rose said.

Charlie stood and made her way over to the counter. After filling up a glass of water, she turned. "Doing what?"

"Living your life in the past." Rose stood and joined Charlie. "I'm old. I'm going to die soon. Most of the time, I don't remember anything. But, I've lived my life. I've loved harder than you can imagine. I'm okay with forgetting."

Charlie's heart sank. She wasn't.

"But, you're young. You deserve that once in a lifetime, mind bending love. You can't keep living your life for me. Or for this place. Penny told me about the bank." Rose reached out and grabbed Charlie's hand. "You need to let these things go. Your granny would have wanted it."

Tears flowed as Charlie glanced around the room. "I can't. I don't know how."

Rose reached up and cradled Charlie's cheek in her hand. "Lean on someone. Let him in and have him take care of *you* for once."

The memory of Mitchell's blue eyes flew into her mind. Those were the exact words he'd said to her.

"But—"

Rose shook her head. "Go. Now. Tell Mitchell how you feel."

Charlie shook her head. "No. Not when you know who I am."

"Yes, now. Let me go. I have Penny and Floyd to take care of me. It's okay." She leaned in and kissed Charlie on the cheek. "Please. Nothing would make me happier than for the two kids I love the most to get together. Leave me this happy memory."

Charlie glanced at Rose then over to Floyd and Penny. They both nodded in agreement.

"I should go?"

Rose began shoving her toward the kitchen door. "Go pack. I'll find his address."

Charlie glanced at them one more time then headed to her room. She flew around, grabbing everything she could think of and shoved them into her suitcase.

When she got back to the kitchen, Rose had a piece of paper in her hand. Penny stood next to her with the polar bear Mitchell had won cradled in her arm.

"This was in his room," she said, handing it toward Charlie followed by a folded-up piece of paper.

Charlie took it and opened the note. She read it, and her heart soared. Perhaps, there was a chance.

"What did it say?" Penny asked.

Charlie folded it and stashed it in her purse. "He hopes someday I can forgive him."

Before anyone could say anything, the back door opened. Charlie's heart pounded, but then slowed when Francis walked in.

"What's going on here?" Francis asked, glancing around.

Charlie stepped forward. "Francis?"

She nodded. "Yes." Then she glanced around the room. "What's happening here?"

"You remember who we are?" Charlie couldn't believe it. Both women remembered on the same day? Her heart soared. "Where have you been?" She nodded toward the outside.

"I was visiting Neil," Francis said as she shut the door.

Charlie grabbed her suitcase. If she didn't do it now, she would lose her nerve. "Well, I'm off to tell Rose's grandson that I love him."

Francis stared at her. "Wow, I've missed so much."

Rose snorted. "You're telling me."

Charlie ran and hugged each woman. "I love you both," she said as she pulled back to smile at them.

Rose patted her arm. "We love you, too. Now go!"

Francis nodded in agreement.

Charlie turned to Penny.

"Yes, go. I've got it covered here," Penny said, waving her hand.

Charlie smiled and headed to the door.

"Thanks for planting those daisies," Francis said as she passed by.

Turning, Charlie furrowed her brow. "What?"

"There're daisies at Neil's grave. Thanks for planting them."

"I didn't..." She breathed out. "Mitchell did it." Suddenly, all she wanted to do was see him. "Bye, guys! I love you."

She raced down the steps and over to her car. All four of the people she loved stood on the porch, waving at her. If only Mitchell was there, her life would be complete.

"Ma'am, like I told you. I can't let you up there without Mr. Kingsley's direct permission," the doorman said as he stared at Charlie.

She sighed and pushed her hand through her hair. "Please, I need to speak to him." She was exhausted from the eight-hour flight. She tried to pump herself up, but the longer she stood there, the faster her confidence fizzled out. She hated the city.

The man held up his hand. "I'm sorry. It's policy."

She sighed. What was she going to do? There was no way she'd find Mitchell at ten o'clock at night in a city this big. "Could you at least tell me if he's there?"

The man narrowed his eyes then turned to his computer. "You can call his assistant. She might know where he is." He waved his hand to the monitor and turned back to greet a man in an expensive looking suit.

Taking her phone out, Charlie punched in the number. Hitting talk, she lifted the phone to her ear and held her breath.

22

MITCHELL

"...*And* that's what I think will be best for the new high-rise you've purchased."

Mitchell stared at the dark liquor in his glass, not really paying attention to the architect across from him. He didn't know what he was thinking, agreeing to have drinks with Ivy. She'd said it was just a business meeting, but from the way she was smiling at him, she wanted more. But all he could do was think about Charlie.

"Mitchell?"

Startled, he glanced up. Crap, she'd finished talking. "I'm sorry." He leaned forward. "You were saying?"

She smiled as she brought her glass to her lips. "Is it a girl?"

He sat straighter in his chair. "Is it that obvious?"

The glass of champagne made a clink as she set it down on the table. "Yes."

He felt like such an idiot. Charlie had made it pretty clear how she felt about him. But here he was, mooning after her. "She basically told me she wants nothing to do with me."

A sympathetic look passed over Ivy's face. "Ooo, that had to hurt."

Mitchell's stomach twisted. "Yeah." He dropped his gaze and scanned the restaurant. A woman with dark brown hair and fair skin caught his attention. She stood twenty feet away with a shocked expression. It looked like... Charlie.

He blinked and sat up further.

Her eyes widened as she glanced from him to Ivy. Her face fell as she turned and sprinted for the door, dragging her luggage behind her.

"Char—Charlie!" Mitchell yelled as he stood and smacked his knee on the table which caused the plates and utensils to jump.

"Charlie? Is that the girl? She's here?" Ivy turned, glancing around.

"Yeah. I have to go," he said as he threw his napkin on the table and grabbed his suit coat.

"Of course, go," she said, waving her hand toward Charlie's retreating frame.

By the time Mitchell got to the door, Charlie had disappeared. He raced through it and onto the sidewalk. Crowds spilt around him as he stood there, debating which way she'd gone. Cursing, he headed to the left, hoping this was the right way.

As he neared the corner, he breathed a sigh of relief. She was standing there, waiting for the walk signal while people weaved around her. New Yorkers didn't wait and Charlie stuck out like a sore thumb. His heart pounded as he approached her.

"Charlie?" He reached out and touched her shoulder.

Whipping around, her eyes widened. "Mitchell?"

He nodded at her. Why was she acting weird? "Why are you here?" Suddenly, dread sank in his stomach. "Is Rose okay?"

Confusion flitted over her face then she nodded. "Yes. Rose is fine. I'm sorry. I didn't mean to scare you."

A disgruntled walker muttered under his breath as he passed by. Mitchell grabbed Charlie's elbow and led her away from the sidewalk and over to stand under a building's awning.

"If Rose is okay, why are you here?"

Charlie fiddled with her purse strap. "I'm so sorry. I didn't know."

Was she talking in code? "Know what?"

"About… her." She nodded in the direction of the restaurant. "When I called Sondra she said you were having dinner. I never imagined…" She peeked over at him.

"What? Ivy? I'm not on a date. She's an architect who's helping with a new building we just bought." His heart picked up speed. Why would it matter to Charlie if he was dating? She'd made it pretty clear that she didn't want anything to do with him. Did he dare hope?

"Oh." Her cheeks flushed as she glanced back to the ground. Then she reached into her purse and pulled out a piece of paper. "I realized I never paid you. You know, for the mattresses." She held out the paper.

He stared down at her check. "I don't want that." He glanced up at her. Really? That's why she'd come?

Her face fell. "Please, I don't feel good about you paying for them."

His stomach twisted. "No. I'm not taking your money."

She chewed her lip. "Mitchell, I…"

He'd had enough of this. "That's why you came here? To pay me? That's what the mail is for. Keep your money. The mattresses were a gift." He turned, hoping she couldn't see his breaking heart.

"Wait," she called out as she grabbed his arm.

He stopped and turned. "What do you want, Charlie?"

She chewed her lip again. He wished she would just come out with it.

"I also wanted to thank you."

Scrubbing his face, Mitchell peered down at her. "For what?"

"Your help with everything. Francis's flowers, finding me when I hit my head, and helping me see how much I don't want Alex in my life." She glanced up at him through her thick lashes.

His heart pounded. "You deserve to be taken care of and Alex isn't the guy to do it."

She nodded. "I know."

Silence fell between them. What was he supposed to do? "Charlie..." He reached out to touch her. She backed up, and his heart sank. How did he keep misreading her?

"Wait. Let me get this out before I lose my nerve." She glanced around for a moment, then back up to Mitchell. "Rose remembered."

Great, and he'd missed it.

As if sensing his disappointment, she furrowed her brow. "I'm sorry. I had no right to force you to go. You should have stayed. She was so happy when we told her you had visited."

He swallowed against the lump in his throat. At least she'd known he had made an effort. "That's good I guess."

Charlie nodded. "While we were talking, I told her about what happened." Her voice dropped. "About us."

Mitchell raised his eyebrows. There was an us?

"I didn't have to tell her. She guessed it on her own." She chewed her lip again.

"Guessed what?"

Charlie took a deep breath. "That I love you."

Mitchell's ears rang. What did she just say? "What?"

She smiled at him. "I love you, and I'm sorry that I treated you the way I did. I was just scared. I got the foreclosure notice from the bank, Rose was sad, and I just wasn't sure I was ready to admit how I felt about you."

He stared at her. She looked so sad and broken. Not waiting for her to speak again, he placed both hands on her cheeks and leaned in. When his lips met hers, his heart soared. They were warm and familiar. Like everything he'd ever wanted. Moving his hands to her waist, he pulled her close to deepen the kiss.

There were a few whistles from people passing by, but Mitchell didn't care. Charlie noticed and giggled as her hands wove their way into his hair. The sensation of having her close to him replaced all the pain he'd felt when she told him to leave. He was never going to let her go.

When they came up for air, Charlie glanced up at him with her lips pink and puffy.

"I love you, Charlie. From the moment you dumped water in my lap." He leaned in and kissed her forehead, both cheeks, and then lightly on her lips.

She smiled up at him. "And I've loved you from the moment you got me fired."

Great. He narrowed his eyes at her. "Can we come up with something more romantic?"

She giggled and reached up to brush her lips against his. "No, because it's ours."

He wrapped his arms around her waist and picked her up. Spinning her around, he laughed as she giggled. This was where he belonged, and he was never going to let her go.

EPILOGUE

The pounding of hammers and nail guns filled the air. Charlie opened her eyes and felt around on the bed. Mitchell was gone.

Sighing, she flipped onto her back and lifted up her hand. Nestled between her fingers was the largest diamond she'd ever seen. Well, it wasn't as big as Victoria's. She wouldn't let Mitchell buy her one that huge.

She still couldn't believe that she was a wife now. They hadn't waited long. Mitchell wanted to keep his promise to Rose, so they were married a month later.

Mitchell spoke with the bank and bought the retirement home as a wedding gift for her. The last few months had consisted of renovations to the place.

Pulling the covers off, Charlie made her way to the new adjacent bathroom. One of the requirements to the remodel was that every room got a bathroom.

Her stomach churned as she glanced at the calendar. Huh, that was strange. She was late. She chewed her lip. It couldn't be. Reaching into her purse, she pulled out a little box. She'd bought it a few weeks back with the hope of needing to use it soon. Ripping it open, she stared at it. Was it wrong to hope?

After she took the test, she sat on the toilet and waited. It took all her strength not to peek over at it. When three minutes passed, she stood. Closing her eyes, she brought the stick up and held it there. Gathering her nerves, she peeked.

There were two pink lines in the window. She sputtered as she stared at it. Could it be? She placed it on the sink. How was she going to tell Mitchell?

Their bedroom door opened.

"Hey, babe, I brought you some water," Mitchell said as he shut the door behind him.

Charlie bolted from the bathroom and into his arms. He laughed and picked her up.

"Wow, I should do that more often," he said. His voice was muffled from her hair.

Leaning back, Charlie smiled at him. "I have a surprise."

Mitchell narrowed his eyes. "What surprise could you have possibly conjured up in the bathroom?"

She wiggled until he set her down then she grabbed his hand. "I'll show you. Close your eyes."

She led him into the bathroom and over to the sink. After picking the test up with a piece of toilet paper, she held it level with his eyes. "You can open them now."

Mitchell obeyed, and he studied it for a moment. His arms surrounded her as he pulled her close. "Is that…"

Charlie nodded. "I'm pregnant."

Before she could say more, he pressed his lips to hers. She giggled and returned his kiss.

He pulled away, glanced over at the test, and kissed her again. "I love you, Mrs. Kingsley."

Charlie stepped back and stared into his eyes. "I love you, Mr. Kingsley."

He hugged her again. "I have a surprise for you," he whispered into her ear.

Charlie leaned back to look at him. "What?"

"Guess who's here."

Charlie's stomach shot to her throat. "Rose?" she whispered.

He nodded. It had been so long since the last time she'd come back to them.

Not wanting to stand around and waste time, she grabbed his hand. "Come on. Let's go tell her."

NEXT IN THE SERIES

The next in the Clean Billionaire Romance series

Forgiving the Billionaire

A Holiday Billionaire Romance

ABOUT THE AUTHOR

Anne-Marie Meyer lives in MN with her family. She loves romantic movies and stories.

See other books by her pen name Amy Linnabary
    The Fairytale Prophecies (a young adult series)
    1. Cinder Heart
    2. Fairest One
    3. Peculiar Beauty
    The Adventure Brothers (a middle grade series)
    1. Save the Bats
    2. Free the Dolphin

anne-mariemeyer.com

JOIN THE NEWSLETTER

Head on over to anne-mariemeyer.com to join the newsletter and receive updates on new releases and sales!

Also, I am working on a novella, Love at the Carnival, that I will be sending out to all my newsletter followers once it is finished.

Manufactured by Amazon.ca
Bolton, ON

34690324R00113